Advance Praise for *Tagging Freedom*

"In *Tagging Freedom*, cousins Kareem and Samira, a Syrian refugee and Syrian American teen, stand up to oppression and bigotry, cope with painful events, and use their voices and their art to make a difference. **This is an important book—a book that shows how art and activism can change the way people see the world and see themselves.**"

—Rajani LaRocca, Newbery Honor and
Walter Award–winning author of *Red, White, and Whole*

"Rhonda Roumani's *Tagging Freedom* is **inspiring, insightful, and a call for action**. The story is an emotional journey of growth, struggle and ultimately triumph!"

—Lisa Moore Ramée, author of
A Good Kind of Trouble and *Something to Say*

"Rhonda Roumani weaves an intimate and powerful middle-grade narrative, delving into the lives of a Syrian boy who valiantly protests for Syria's freedom and a Syrian girl navigating the complexities of her identity and heritage. In a country torn by turmoil, their artistic pursuits become a form of protest, amplifying their voices and igniting hope in the hearts of those around them. **Roumani captures the transformative nature of art and its ability to inspire change, making this a captivating and empowering tale for young readers. A must read.**"

—Zoulfa Katouh, author of *As Long as the Lemon Trees Grow*

"Rhonda Roumani's debut novel *Tagging Freedom* is a much-needed story with an authentic and heartbreaking perspective on the Syrian crisis. Roumani seamlessly weaves two characters' points of view, creating a compelling story. **Tagging Freedom will inspire readers to be proud of their identities, step into their own light, and most important, create change.**"

—Reem Faruqi, award-winning author of
Unsettled, Golden Girl, and *Call Me Adnan*

"*Tagging Freedom* masterfully brings to light tragic and turbulent events in recent history through the eyes of Syrian Kareem and his American cousin Samira. **It's a raw and relatable story of friendship, acceptance, and the desire within all of us to express ourselves and live freely.** I'm grateful this thoughtful and hope-filled book exists—and I couldn't put it down!"

—Hena Khan, author of *Amina's Voice*

TAGGING FREEDOM

RHONDA ROUMANI

union
square
kids

NEW YORK

union
square
kids

NEW YORK

ISBN 978-1-4549-5071-4 (hardcover)
ISBN 978-1-4549-5072-1 (paperback)
ISBN 978-1-4549-5073-8 (e-book)

Library of Congress Cataloging-in-Publication Data

Names: Roumani, Rhonda, author.
Title: Tagging freedom / by Rhonda Roumani.
Description: New York : Union Square Kids, 2023. | Audience: Ages 8–12. |
Summary: Set in the early days of the Syrian Civil War, cousins Kareem and
Samira living in Massachusetts navigate the growing conflict in Syria,
new friendships, and the use of art to express themselves.
Identifiers: LCCN 2023001259 (print) | LCCN 2023001260 (ebook) |
ISBN 9781454950714 (hardcover) | ISBN 9781454950721 (trade paperback) |
ISBN 9781454950738 (epub)
Subjects: CYAC: Cousins—Fiction. | Graffiti—Fiction. | Syrian Americans—Fiction. |
Syrians—Massachusetts—Fiction. | Syria—History—Civil War, 2011—Fiction. |
BISAC: JUVENILE FICTION / People & Places / United States /
Middle Eastern & Arab American | JUVENILE FICTION / Art
Classification: LCC PZ7.1.R7675 Tag 2023 (print) |
LCC PZ7.1.R7675 (ebook) | DDC [E]—dc23
LC record available at https://lccn.loc.gov/2023001259
LC ebook record available at https://lccn.loc.gov/2023001260

For information about custom editions, special sales, and premium purchases,
please contact specialsales@unionsquareandco.com.

Printed in the United States of America
Lot #:
2 4 6 8 10 9 7 5 3 1
09/23

unionsquareandco.com

Cover art by Sara Alfageeh
Cover and interior design by Melissa Farris

To Mama and Baba,
For bringing Syria into our home,
and our hearts, even when it was so far away.
I love you.

CHAPTER 1

Kareem

Damascus, Syria

Kareem picked up the black spray paint and studied the sandy-colored wall.

"We need fifteen white birds, Yusuf," he whispered loudly. "There's only fourteen white ones."

The moonlight reflected gently off the fresh white paint as Yusuf stepped back and started counting. Kareem turned a trash can over and quickly climbed onto it, using his arms for balance as he straightened his tall, thin frame.

"Ala mahlak, Kareem," whispered Yusuf. "Don't fall."

"Ya, Yusuf! Kareem's right," called Hassan from the other side of the building. "There are only fourteen white ones."

"Shh, too loud, Hassan," said Kareem in a hushed yell. "Get back to your position. Focus on the street."

"I'm watching, I'm watching." Hassan looked around the corner of the building and took a deep breath of his inhaler. "It's still clear. Yalla, hurry up. You're taking too long."

"Hassan, khalas," said George, who was the lookout on the other side. "You guys are good. There's sixteen minutes before the adhan. You got this!"

Yusuf got back to work, while Kareem shook the black can and looked at the other birds, each one the size of two outstretched palms.

Twice as big. The black one has to be the biggest. It is THE one.

Kareem raised his arm high, the other hand carefully placed so as not to touch the wet white paint. He sprayed a large quarter circle, the length of two of the other birds' wingspans. Some of the white birds had wings that were extended, others had wings that were in mid-flap. They'd spent the day before creating stencils to help it all go faster. But Kareem would free-spray the black one. It was the most important, and it had to soar high above the others.

Carefully, he created a row of delicate feathers. Then, the rear of the bird's body, its feet peeking out beneath, and the other wing. Finally, feathers again. Kareem tucked the can inside his coat and took out the red can he'd used for the words that ran through the middle of the wall. He sprayed a heart around the black bird.

"Done." Kareem looked up at the lonely black bird flying above the rest. "Hamza's done." He jumped off the trash can, his fingers tingling with excitement. "This is the one, guys. Let's sign it."

Hassan ran over, his eyes wide. "Are you *kidding* me? No. 'We deserve to fly FREE.' That's it."

"No one will understand the birds are the Dara'a boys if we don't tag it. Or that the black bird is Hamza." Kareem shook the black can and locked eyes with Hassan. "Hashtag, we stand with Dara'a or hashtag, we are all Hamza. Which one?"

"You *know* that's too risky. 'We deserve to fly FREE' does the job. It's what we *all* agreed on," said Hassan, wiping beads of sweat off his forehead.

"Yalla, we're out," came a deep voice from around the corner. Ramy swooped in, picked up an extra paint can near Hassan's feet, and stuffed it into his jacket. "Yalla, yalla. Go. No time. Out."

Ramy's orders fell on Kareem's ears like a piano's staccato: sharp and fast. He and Yusuf instantly fell silent. Without another word, each boy went in a different direction, just as they had planned.

Kareem walked quickly south, toward a mosque that was just a few blocks away, his entire body buzzing with excitement. Ramy, Yusuf's sixteen-year-old brother, had helped them plan it all—down to the smallest detail. The mural, the location, the stencils, the getaway.

He wasn't supposed to look back at the building. That was another part of their plan. But he couldn't help it. He took a quick peek over his shoulder to admire their newly painted wall from afar.

It was perfect. Beautiful. Kareem wished he could take a picture. But if the mukhabarat found the pictures on his phone, it would be over. Immediate proof of guilt. Kareem closed his eyes and imagined the click of his phone's camera. A mental picture would have to do.

Kareem turned around and stuffed his hands into his jacket pockets as he rounded a corner.

"Slow down, slow down," he mumbled to himself. Now he was on his way to fajr prayer, not escaping a crime scene. Just a few weeks ago, a piece like this would have been unimaginable in Damascus. But there it was, in bright, bold letters: We deserve to FLY FREE. He wanted to jump up and down, wave his arms, and yell at the top of his lungs that the birds were the graffiti boys from Dara'a, and the black one was Hamza. If people knew, it would mean so much more. That's what it would feel like to *really* be free.

But they weren't. Not yet. This was what the revolution was about. Why they were protesting. Why they were graffitiing.

And why Hamza had died.

He picked up his pace again and took in a deep breath of the crisp, morning Damascus air. He wondered whether Hassan had reached the other mosque, or if Ramy and Yusuf had dropped George off at home yet. He checked his phone for their coded messages. Nothing.

Allahu Akbar, Allahu Akbar.

The adhan blared from the minaret overhead, just as Kareem reached the mosque's front gate. He looked down at his shoes and noticed a splatter of black paint on the top corner of his bright blue sneakers. His heart sped up. Had the guard noticed when he walked up to the mosque's gates? He couldn't turn back now. That would look suspicious. He took his shoes off and slid them into a cubby.

He stepped onto the soft rug and joined a small group of men getting ready to pray. His phone vibrated in his pocket.

It's probably Hassan. He should have arrived at his mosque first.

Kareem took a quick peek at his phone.

Hassan

Finished studying. Night.

Kareem nodded. Hassan was safe. He quickly slid the phone's keyboard out and typed.

Kareem

See you at school. ☺

Kareem prayed with the other men and then sat back on his feet for a moment, thinking about what they had just accomplished. This was the most exciting thing he had ever done. The Dara'a boys had done the same thing, just outside their school, a mere hour south from where he was. How had the security services discovered that they were the ones who had graffitied their school? Had someone seen them? Had the boys taken precautions? Some of those boys were just twelve and thirteen years old, the same age as Kareem and his friends. They had been caught and tortured. Hamza wasn't one of the graffiti boys. Hamza was detained a week later when he attended a protest with his family. But unlike the Dara'a boys, Hamza never came home. Kareem had seen his picture. Hamza could have been any of his classmates. Rosy, chubby cheeks. Brown eyes. A sweet smile.

What if George or Hassan had been Hamza? What if I had been Hamza?

His throat and body tightened with fear. He recited a small prayer for the boys and then for Hamza. He asked Allah to protect the protesters. They were out in droves now. This time was different. They wouldn't get arrested. That's what Ramy had explained to them. The revolution needed the masses to protect the one. They had to resist *because* of Hamza. Because Hamza couldn't anymore.

He got up, grabbed his shoes, and followed the crowd out of the mosque. His phone vibrated again.

George

Why would you text us that this early?

Yusuf

Seriously. Shoo ghaleez.

Hassan

I am not annoying!

Kareem nodded. They were safe. If only they could have tagged their work. But he knew it wouldn't stay up for long. The security forces would paint over it soon.

"Almost perfect," he whispered to himself as he walked home, imagining it with the Hamza hashtag. "Insha'Allah, next time."

CHAPTER 2

Samira

Allansdale, MA

Sam fixed her curls in her locker mirror and slammed the door shut. She needed to find Eleanora and get her to the art room before the Spirit Squad arrived.

As if she'd been summoned, Ellie appeared out of nowhere. "Let's get out of here." She slid her arm in Sam's and guided her toward the school's exit. "Nana said her famous rugelach would be ready right after school. I've been drooling all afternoon thinking about the flaky, buttery goodness and sticky apricot jam."

Sam had spent most of last period rehearsing her five-point spiel in her head, but she knew convincing her best friend wasn't going to be easy. "Okay, we just have to make a quick stop first." She tugged Ellie in a different direction. "Shouldn't take more than an hour."

"An hour? That's not quick, Sam. Where are we going?"

"We just need to attend this . . . umm . . . meeting, and then it'll be rugelach time." Sam gave Ellie the biggest, roundest, most desperate eyes she could muster. But doe eyes didn't usually work on Ellie, so Sam moved on to plan B: brute force. She nudged Ellie toward the stairwell, maneuvering her around pods of kids talking in the hallway and a large group coming out of a classroom.

"Samira Sukkari," said Ellie, digging her heels into the waxy linoleum floor. "What's going on? Why are you giving me that look? I'm not your dad. Those eyes don't work on me."

Sam sighed. She had wanted to get Ellie to the art room before she had to explain. The element of surprise had been her best hope. If Ellie knew what was going on, she'd never agree to it.

"I was invited to join Spirit Squad, and I want you to join, too," Sam blurted out.

Ellie's face reddened, and she slowly mouthed, "No way."

Sam fast-tracked to emergency step five: begging.

"Please, please, please. Please, Ellie. I need this. And I need you there. I can't do this without you."

"How can you join Spirit Squad?" Ellie looked Sam directly in the eyes. "After what they did to you in fourth grade?"

"Fourth grade was three years ago! Anyway, Lucy invited me, not Cat. Cat was there, but Lucy asked me to join. She's so nice, and she wasn't even here in fourth grade! I'm meant for Spirit Squad, Ellie. You know how much I love cheering and chanting and singing." Sam started jumping around to demonstrate. Ellie just stood there with her hands on her hips, her blue bangs barely covering her eye rolls. "I already started painting a banner for the big game. I need your help with it. I promise I won't splatter paint on you this time. And it won't take long. Half an hour tops, I promise."

"Splatter paint? You started a full-on paint war last time!" said Ellie, half smiling despite her attempt to glare. "We got in so much trouble."

"Yeah, that's what I said," said Sam, her eyes brightening. "I won't splatter paint on you. By mistake."

Sam held her breath. This wasn't how she had imagined it all coming out. In her math class daydream, Sam had delivered her carefully worded, five-point explanation and then Ellie had said, "Of course, Sam, anything for my best friend." Then they'd practically skipped to room 245 together. Fine, she knew that wasn't going to happen, but Sam had still hoped for a more positive reaction than this. She mustered a desperate grin.

"It's still Cat's squad," said Ellie. "She's not a nice person. She's using you, Sam, or planning something. That's the only reason she'd let you join. And you know it."

"Come on, Ellie." If there were fewer people around, Sam would have thrown herself at Ellie's feet. Sometimes pure comedic, please-make-this-embarrassing-moment-stop tactics worked on her.

"Do what you want, Sam, but I can't watch you go through this again. I won't."

Sam's stomach fell as she watched her best friend walk away. She wanted to yell, "But I need you, Eleanora Gold," like they did in the movies. But this wasn't the movies. It was her life. And her best friend had just deserted her.

Sam continued to the art room alone. Her hands slipped on the door handle and her stomach lurched as she settled herself into a chair. Soon, Lucy, Cat, Avery, and the others would walk through the same doors and now she was a big, hot mess. Normally, Sam did everything she could to avoid them. But after her talk with Lucy, she had decided that today was the day everything was going to change for her at Allansdale Middle School. She was tired of worrying about what would happen at school each day, of trying to be invisible. But she had planned on having Ellie by her side. She needed her by her side. Sam took in a deep breath and grabbed the rolled-up banner and paint supplies.

Please, please, please let this go smoothly.

She scooped some red paint into a paint well and mixed in the orange and yellow. "I don't need you anyway, Eleanora Gold," she muttered, pulling a container of sugar-coated garbanzo beans from her bag and popping one into her mouth. She examined the hue she'd created, then added a bit more orange. "You don't get it. You could live like a hermit in the Arctic with only a school of penguins for friends, and you'd be totally fine."

She should have known better than to ask Ellie to join.

"She's using you." Sam mimicked Ellie as she unrolled the banner. "That's the only reason she'd let you join . . . blah blah blah. ARGH."

Maybe Ellie was right, but Sam was tired of feeling like she didn't fit in anywhere. She just wanted to be herself again. She *belonged* in Spirit Squad. Ellie might think it was fake and shallow, but it wasn't just a cheer squad. It was a cheer, dance, art, singing, and spirit squad, all rolled into one. And Sam loved cheering and chanting and dancing and singing and banner making and making new friends. Being a part of Spirit Squad meant you were definitely part of AMS. Spirit Squad *was* AMS. The only reason Sam had never joined was because of Cat Spencer. Fourth grade had changed everything.

Sam pushed away the tiny Tupperware of pastel-colored beans and refocused her attention on the banner.

The letters are all wrong.

She redrew the letters—R-O-A-R—on the large cloth banner draped over the table, then stepped back to examine them. The font was exactly what she'd envisioned. Fierce, but confident. The bottoms of the letters had a toothy quality, and she had created a modern, mane-like effect with the rounded part of the Rs.

Allansdale: Hear us ROAR.

The words surrounded a pouncing lion with its mouth wide open. Above, in block letters, it read BOYS SOCCER REGIONAL QUARTERFINALS. She still had to draw 2011, but she hadn't yet imagined how it would look.

In third grade, Sam had watched a show about people with synesthesia. Instead of hearing or seeing the way most people did, they saw things as colors, or experienced a smell as a shape. Sam didn't think she had synesthesia exactly, but it was the closest thing she had come across that described how she saw the world. Sam saw people as unique fonts. Some were computerized, while others were hand drawn. They could be bubble-like, wavy and beautiful, or straight and constrained. Sam would sketch people's letters in her notebook, sometimes with a manga-style drawing of the person. Those letters became her secret code.

Sam looked at the lion and wished Ellie was with her again. If Ellie helped, the banner would be epic. Ellie was the art *yin* to Sam's *yang*. When they'd made banners for the soup kitchen and animal shelter where Ellie volunteered, she'd drawn the image, and Sam had created the words. They'd chosen the colors together. It was like they spoke their own art language.

Ellie's was an honest type of lettering that said it like it was. At first, Sam thought Ellie's letters were so thin and brittle, they might crumble under the weight of other people's worries. In reality, they were clear, almost mirror-like. Her font was short, crisp, and boxy, but its taller letters reached high above the middle line.

But they were also *so* stubborn.

"OH. MY. GOSH! That's so cool." Avery arrived with Lucy and Cat right behind her. "Take a look!"

"I told you," said Lucy. "Sam's the best! I've seen her stuff in art. It's amazing."

"Thanks." Sam's face burned bright red.

"Thanks for doing this for us," said Lucy, beaming. "See, Cat? She's perfect for this."

Cat stood silently at the head of the table, assessing the banner like a judge in a competition. Sam's throat tightened as she waited for the verdict. She had tried to draw Cat's letters on a number of occasions but could never quite get them right. They were always missing something. Sam needed the manga drawing to complete her caricature: a girl in a flying, punching pose, with a high, platinum-white ponytail and icy blue eyes. No lettering had done the job.

"You forgot the 2011," said Cat. "And to write 'Spirit Squad' down at the bottom. People need to know it's ours."

"Oh yeah, I'm still working on that," Sam mumbled, lowering her eyes.

"What can we do?" Lucy grabbed a chair. "Put us to work, Sam!"

Sam's heart fluttered. She wasn't sure why she was so nervous, except that Cat just stood there stone-faced, occasionally texting. This was why she'd wanted Ellie with her. Ellie calmed her. She wasn't just her best friend. She was her safety net.

"Lucy, you can start on the first R. Avery, maybe start on the one at the other end so you won't get in each other's way." Sam paused and glanced at Cat. "Be careful not to go over the lines. Clean lines will make it look really good."

"Hey, what are these?" Lucy peered at the pastel pink and blue garbanzo beans, then popped one in her mouth. "They're weird, but sorta good."

Sam had completely forgotten to put away her stash of adameh ala succar. She hadn't planned on introducing them to anybody at school.

"They're, uhh, they're sugar-coated chickpeas." Sam reached for the Tupperware bowl but knocked it over in her rush. The little balls rolled over the banner, some sticking to the wet paint as Sam frantically tried to collect them. Cat and Avery snickered behind her.

"Sugar-coated chickpeas?" Cat said. "That doesn't even make sense!"

Sam turned even redder. "They're Syrian," she said softly. "My mom says they're good for you."

"Cat, they're actually pretty good. Here." Lucy held out a pink one. "They're a little chalky, but they're sweet. It sort of tastes like flowers."

"I'll try it," said Avery. She popped it in her mouth and chewed for a few seconds as everyone stared. Then, she hurried to the sink, grabbed a paper towel, and spit out the soggy mess. She looked at Sam apologetically. "Sorry. Uh, they're definitely chalky . . . or something."

Sam's stomach dropped. She wished the others had never seen the treats. Why on earth would they eat something that wasn't theirs?

15

Cat scrunched her nose at the adameh ala succar. "I'm not into chalky chickpeas. But I'll help paint."

Flooded with relief, Sam handed Cat a brush.

Note to self: bring more normal snacks next time.

"This is going to look so good," said Lucy, popping a few more of the sweet chickpeas in her mouth. "I can't wait for everybody to see it!"

Sam loosened her grip on her brush and smiled at Lucy. "Neither can I." She filled in the O with the bright reddish-orange paint. She bit her lip as Cat painted over the clean edges she'd warned them about. She would have to fix it with white once it dried, but it would be okay. Sam was part of Spirit Squad now, that's what mattered. Things were going to be great.

CHAPTER 3

KAREEM

Kareem and Hassan locked arms. Yusuf ran to Hassan's right and slid his arm through Hassan's, while George took Kareem's left. The tightly linked quartet marched among a sea of strangers.

The ground beneath Kareem vibrated as thousands of feet hit the pavement. A banner fluttered above the crowd: WE WANT FREEDOM FOR ALL. Tetas and jiddos, mothers and fathers, and little kids seated on their parents' shoulders chanted in unison.

He, Kareem Haddad, was protesting *in* Syria. The only "protests" Kareem had ever seen before in person were staged by the government. If anyone had told him a few weeks earlier that thousands would take to the streets of Damascus to demand that President Bashar al-Assad step down, he would never have believed it. For years, the mukhabarat had kept Syrians afraid. People whispered because informants were everywhere. They were taxi drivers and garbage collectors, friends, or even an aunt or uncle. In Damascus, people said that "even

the walls have ears." The mukhabarat were nowhere and everywhere at once.

So everybody kept quiet.

Now, here they were, arms locked, marching through
Damascus, chanting at the top of their lungs. They'd told a
lie to get there, but they had agreed it was a necessary lie. And
Ramy had convinced them they had to be there, even if their
parents forbade it.

"Listen, ya shabab," Ramy had said, towering over them in
Yusuf's room. They'd been playing rounds of one-on-one Nerf
basketball, but Ramy had demolished them with his six-foot
frame. "We're supposed to listen to our parents. I always listen
to mine. But . . ."

Ramy sat down on a bed next to Kareem and continued.

"There are times, moments in life, we have to follow our
beliefs. This is one of those times. To change this country, we
have to show up. All of us. If we all listened to our parents, the
whole country would stay home, afraid."

"It's a *good* lie!" Yusuf had exclaimed, laughing.

"Come on, Yusuf," Hassan had pushed back. He scrunched
his nose and blinked feverishly, the way he did when he was
nervous. "What if something happens while we're there? They'll
kill us. I mean, our parents will, not the mukhabarat. Let's just
tell them we want to go."

"Hassan!" Yusuf yelled back. "We already talked about this.
If you tell your parents, our parents will find out. And we already

know that my parents and Kareem's parents are not okay with us going."

The boys had argued until Hassan caved. Ramy calmed Hassan down by promising to keep an eye on them, just like his parents would if they were there.

So they'd told their parents they were doing what they normally did on a Friday afternoon, when a revolution wasn't taking place in their backyard—playing a pickup game of soccer at the nadi followed by shawarma sandwiches. Instead, they marched.

Ramy's voice echoed over the bullhorn: "Al Sha'ab Youreed Isqaat al Nizam." He smiled over his shoulder and pounded his fist in Kareem's direction, and Kareem smiled back. He had always wanted an older brother like Ramy. Kareem repeated the chant, squeezing his elbow to bring Hassan closer. At the ends, Yusuf and George thrust their free fists in the air to the beat of the chant. "Al Sha'ab Youreed Isqaat al Nizam . . . Al Sha'ab Youreed Isqaat al Nizam."

He'd first heard the chant on television when Tunisians rose up against their dictator. Then came the Egyptian revolution. Syrians secretly tuned in to the news to cheer on the largest country in the Arab world as they chanted those very same lines. Kareem watched every night, as if it was the World Cup of revolutions. He and his parents couldn't help but root for the millions—no, *tens of millions*—who flooded Tahrir Square, waving Egyptian flags and chanting, "The people want to overthrow the government."

At the time, Kareem believed the same thing could never happen in Syria. Syrians were too scared. Egyptians could at least tell jokes about their president. Kareem's own parents laughed at memes poking fun of Egyptian president Hosni Mubarak, but no one told jokes about Bashar al-Assad. There weren't any.

Then, the unthinkable happened. The fifteen boys from Dara'a graffitied their school's walls.

It's your turn, Doctor.

They tagged the wall for the entire town to see. Fifteen boys between ten and fifteen dared to write what others were too scared to even think. The doctor was Syrian president Bashar al-Assad, an ophthalmologist by training.

No one was sure exactly why the boys did it. It was the kind of thing that people secretly thought, but no one actually dared to voice. Some people said they were just imitating what they saw on television. Others said they were just boys being boys. What teenager wouldn't want to paint on walls? Others said one boy's mother was an activist herself and that her son had been the ringleader.

The following day, local authorities arrested the boys. They were tortured. Protests erupted around Dara'a, demanding that the boys be released. A few weeks later, during one of the protests, another boy named Hamza was arrested. He died in custody.

That was when Syria's streets erupted, when Syrians finally decided enough was enough. It was one thing to arrest adults; an entirely different thing to arrest, torture, and murder children.

When Kareem heard about Hamza and the other boys, he couldn't get their story out of his head.

A few days later, Kareem and his friends went out to get ice cream at a nearby shop when they noticed random words graffitied on a wall. Freedom in English, Houriyeh in Arabic. When they got home, Yusuf had whispered to Kareem that he thought Ramy might be behind it. He'd seen spray cans in his room.

Kareem couldn't stop thinking about graffiti after that. He loved to paint and draw. He *loved* the idea of creating beautiful artwork on public walls. It was the most visible, most public canvas an artist could ask for. Kareem didn't want to go to museums to see art. He desperately wanted to paint in broad daylight for all to see. He convinced Hassan, George, and Yusuf that they had to do this together.

Kareem and Yusuf started small, just single words. "Freedom." "Justice." Next came phrases: "Free Syria, Freedom Now!" "No Justice, No Peace." Then they researched graffiti online, and saw magnificent pieces from around the world.

That's when they started to think bigger.

Together, Kareem, Yusuf, Hassan, and George had come up with the birds. They'd told Ramy about it, bursting with excitement, and the look of surprise on his face had made

Kareem feel so proud. Ramy said he'd come along to keep them safe. But when they talked about tagging their work, Hassan and Ramy had drawn the line at adding #WeAreAllHamza.

"Inta majnoun?" Hassan had yelled. "It's one thing to leave it vague, to draw birds and write 'freedom.' That will get us in trouble. But to say it's Hamza? My mom won't let me say his name, in our own home. That'll get us killed, like him."

They stood there, in complete silence, as though the air had been sucked out of the room. Then Kareem blurted, "But what's the point of a revolution if you follow all the rules? Isn't that what you told us, Ramy? That we have to spray OUT-SIDE the lines if we're going to change anything?"

He knew that Hassan was right. But he was right, too. Hassan was always scared. He was always the last one to ride his bike down a steep hill or take part in a prank. He never wanted to do anything risky.

Now, marching in the streets together, Kareem glanced over at Hassan belting the newest chant—"Yalla, Irhal, ya Bashar!"—and joined along.

Wow, they were straight up asking Bashar al-Assad to leave. Kareem's heart filled with pride. If only his parents could see this, if only they could experience the excitement. He suddenly wished it would never end. Was this what freedom felt like?

They marched past an abandoned building, right before a bridge. Someone had obviously started construction on it once upon a time, but they had stopped midway. Kareem had noticed it before, but for the first time, he admired its large tan outfacing wall. It was the perfect canvas.

He nudged Hassan, motioning with his head toward the building. He leaned in and whispered, "Graffiti—ala il binayeh houneek."

Hassan shook his head. "No. Too risky."

But Kareem knew he could change Hassan's mind. Hassan was always the point of last resistance—once he was on board, they'd be ready to go. The wall was huge, visible from so many different angles, exposed and yet hidden. It was perfect.

Hassan froze up, while Kareem freed his left arm and pounded his fist in the air as the next chant started.

"Allah, Souriyah, Houriyah ou Bas. Allah, Souriyah, Houriyah ou Bas."

CHAPTER 4

SAMĪRA

Sam checked the clock and sighed.

11:23 a.m.

Another half hour. ARGH.

She rubbed her eyes and yawned. Sunday mornings were brutal. Her parents dragged her out of bed at seven thirty a.m., stuffed a hot cheese sandwich in her hand, then drove her nearly forty minutes to the Islamic Center for a two-hour-long Qur'anic recitation and Arabic class.

A green M&M smacked Sam's cheek. Her other best friend, Layla, was picking them out of a bag under the table. Spending time with Layla was the major redeeming factor of Sunday school. Sister Suzanne stood a few feet away, her laser pointer moving from right to left as the class repeated the lines of Arabic after her.

"Hey, that hurt!" Sam whispered. She threw the M&M back at Layla. "Are you still on the green ones?"

"Uh-huh." Layla smiled. "Still on my Muslim M&M's."

Layla always ate M&M's in color order. She started with the greens, which she dubbed the Muslim ones after a teacher told them green was the color of Islam. "How on earth could a religion have a color?" Layla had blurted, laughing. Next, she ate the yellows, which she called the happy, sunny ones; then the blues and reds, the Americans; and lastly, the brown ones because, "well, we're brown," she explained. It didn't really make sense, but Layla often made no sense. It was what Sam loved about her.

Layla's letters were a solid, pretty cursive; clear, admired by kids and adults alike. Some would even say classic, teacher-perfect script. But most people didn't notice the way the bottoms of her capital letters mischievously tickled the lowercase ones. *That* was what Sam loved about Layla: her ability to still be silly and quirky under that perfect exterior.

Layla popped a few more M&M's in her mouth and sat straighter, just as Sister Suzanne stopped speaking.

"Come on, this won't end." Sam wrapped her arms around her head. "Why won't it end?"

"Okay, Miss Drama Queen," Layla whispered, kicking her underneath the table. "You're gonna get us in trouble."

"Samira, Layla." Sister Suzanne peered at them over her glasses. (She was definitely a strict font: print, straight up and down, between the lines, no flair of any kind. Courier.) "Are you paying attention? We're on Surat Al-Nisaa, Aya 62. Yalla, open your Qur'ans. Samira, please read."

Sam sighed and pulled her Qur'an closer. She hated reading in front of people. Not because she wasn't good at it—last year, she won the annual Qur'an recitation competition. Her father had spent hours with her working on pronunciation. But she worried about what people might say, or kids laughing at her *because* she was good.

When Sam finished, Sister Suzanne moved on to another student. Layla slyly moved closer to Sam.

"Are you coming for pizza with us after class?"

"No, I have to work on a banner for the boys' soccer quarterfinals for Spirit Squad," Sam whispered back. "Want to help?"

"Spirit Squad?" Layla scrunched her eyebrows and shoulders, as if they were invisibly linked, then fanned out her fingers. Sam called this "Arabic sign language." Little motions—flicks of the hand, a bat of the eyelashes or raising of the eyebrow— that imparted whole sentences without uttering a single word. This one meant: What? Spirit Squad? I'm confused. "Isn't Ellie helping?"

"Nah, she's so annoying. And judgy. We might be in a fight. I'm not sure." It didn't exactly feel like a fight at the time, but Sam found herself getting more and more upset as the weekend passed. They usually texted constantly, but neither of them had sent a single text all weekend.

Layla furrowed her brows and pursed her lips. She really knew how to work those eyebrows.

"Okay, girls," said Sister Suzanne, eyeing Sam and Layla disapprovingly. "Everybody, pack up. Prayer is in fifteen minutes. Don't forget to do page fifty-eight and keep working on memorizing Surah Nuh, please."

On the way to the prayer hall, Sam pulled a scarf from her bag and wrapped it around her head and shoulders. "So? Can you help?" she asked. "Please, please, please."

"Sorry, Sam," said Layla, struggling with her own hijab. "I promised the others we'd get pizza, and we're going to a movie. I figured you'd be in." She paused. "What's happening with you and Ellie?"

"Did I mention how judgy she is?" Sam rolled her eyes. "*So* ridiculous."

She wasn't exactly mad at Ellie, more annoyed. They normally did all their banners and posters for Ellie's different causes together. But she wasn't about to apologize when she hadn't done anything wrong. Ellie was the one who had totally overreacted.

Sam explained the whole thing to Layla as they placed their shoes in the cubbies, crossed the rows of soft, plush carpets to the back of the room, and took a seat against a wall. Layla huddled up next to Sam so they could whisper.

"Cat Spencer?" asked Layla. "*The* Cat Spencer? The girl who ruined your life in fourth grade?"

"That's the one." Sam ran the end of her scarf through her fingers. "But I think she's changed, Layla. And you have to meet Lucy. She's great. She's new and . . . so nice."

Layla hesitated and gazed at a framed picture of a grand mosque in the corner of the room as if noticing it for the first time.

"Sam, Cat Spencer literally turned every girl against you," Layla whispered as the room filled with girls and women. "You were so miserable. Remember how she imitated your walk in fourth grade? And then she got all the boys to call you Unibrow Sam in fifth grade. And the rumors she spread . . . ?"

Of course Sam remembered. How could she forget? Friends she'd known for years had turned against her overnight, and she'd spent almost an entire year clueless as to why. She had no idea Cat had gone around telling classmates that Sam had said terrible things behind their backs.

"But, Layla, that's the past. We're in seventh grade now. And *Lucy's* the one who invited me." Sam's hands got sweaty, and she suddenly wished she hadn't said anything. Layla was acting just like Ellie. She didn't understand that this was Sam's chance to make things right again. "Ellie should be making the banner with me, no matter who it's for. I would do it for her."

Layla softly said, "Okay, but remember how she stood up to Cat in the cafeteria in front of the entire fifth and sixth grade, calling her an insecure, mean, lying turd? She was so mad about how Cat was treating you. I bet she's just worried about you."

The memory of Ellie, her spine straight and her cheeks pink with anger, yelling at Cat in front of everyone, softened Sam. Ellie always had her back. She just needed to talk to her again, explain to Ellie how she felt and how she had really needed her there for support. Maybe Ellie would change her mind when she saw how nice Lucy and the other girls were. It wouldn't be easy, though. She was a stubborn font, after all.

"So, want to come to the game on Friday when they hang my banner?" Sam said, changing the subject. "You'll love it. I'm so psyched!"

"I have drama practice," said Layla. "I'm sorry. I'll come to the next one."

Sam sighed. She wished, again, that Layla went to her school. Then Sam wouldn't be the only Muslim *and* the only Arab. She wouldn't always feel so different.

It wasn't that Ellie didn't understand her. In many ways, Ellie understood Sam more than Layla did. Sure, Sam had to explain Ramadan and Eid and why she wasn't allowed to sleep over at friends' houses. But those things weren't that strange to Ellie. She was Jewish and had her own holidays and rules. That was automatic bonding right there.

But with Layla, Sam didn't have to explain anything. They had the same "rules" to complain about. No sleepovers, no boyfriends, no short skirts, no R-rated movies. If Layla went to her school, maybe the giant crater between Sam's home life and school life wouldn't feel so wide.

Even though Ellie and Layla were Sam's best friends, they barely knew each other. They knew *about* each other, but they occupied different worlds. Layla was part of Sam's Muslim-home world; Ellie was part of her outside school world. And they rarely overlapped.

"The real question is, are you excited about the banner or is it because Dylan's going to be there?" Layla grinned. "Isn't he the star player?"

Sam blushed, deeply regretting telling Layla all her secrets. "Layla! That's totally not it." After a moment she added, "Okay, he *might* be there. I mean, yes, he'll be there. But I swear this is about Spirit Squad!"

"Do your parents know about zis Zpirit Zquad?" asked Layla with a big smile. "*Shoo hada? What is zis zpirit zquad?*" Layla shook a hand in the air and raised her left eyebrow, perfectly imitating Sam's dad.

Sam laughed. "Well, I haven't exactly told them about it yet. I just said I'm helping with art projects at school. Which isn't exactly *not* true?"

Sam knew she was stretching the truth, but she also knew her parents would never agree to Spirit Squad. When she'd brought it up last year, they'd said, "We don't waste our time with silly cheerleading." Sam explained it wasn't cheerleading, but her father just shook his head and said, "End of discussion."

"Ahh," said Layla. "I see."

"We make posters and go to some games. We do cheers. That's all."

A wave of guilt came over Sam, but she couldn't tell her parents about Spirit Squad. And that was their fault, not hers. The name made them automatically imagine movies with pom-poms, short skirts, and girls and boys kissing. They didn't understand that kids in school were finally noticing her as an artist. Most parents would be proud.

"I know, habibti. I know." Layla patted Sam's arm. "At least they don't know about Dylan. *That* would be a problem."

"I guess it doesn't hurt that he'll be there," said Sam, playing with a tassel that hung from her hijab.

"Hurt? No." Layla gave her a cartoonish wink. "Flirting with Dylan will be painless."

"Ha-ha. I think something's in your eye, Layla Hamdan."

"Okay, Samira-the-weirda," Layla said as the call to prayer sounded. "Yalla, let's go." She helped Sam up, and they joined the women who'd formed a line for prayer.

Layla was the only person who was allowed to call her Samira or make fun of her name. A boy at school, John Paine, had taunted her with Samira-the-weirda in third grade and it still stung—but not when Layla said it.

"Time to ask Allah to get you through all this," said Layla. "Don't worry, I'll pray that Cat Spencer miraculously turns into my sweet Khalto Mariam or something. Miracles can happen!"

As they started the prayer, Sam thought of Cat and Lucy and Avery and Ellie. "God, please let things go back to how they were before fourth grade," Sam mumbled. She lifted her hands to her head to start her prayer, then placed them over her chest. *Please, ya Allah. Please.*

CHAPTER 5

KAREEM

Kareem dropped his backpack on the couch and walked into the kitchen to find his mom and dad, seated at the table, stuffing zucchinis. For two days straight, he had been quietly chanting *Allah, Souriyah, Houriyah ou Bas* under his breath. The excitement of the protest had still not worn off.

In the kitchen, the voice of Sabah Fakhri singing "Ya Mal el-Sham" blared from the sound system.

Oh treasure of Damascus, come, my treasure
It has been so long, come to me, my beauty

"Are you serious?" Kareem teased, as he grabbed a piping hot cheese fatayer from the counter. "Don't you two get tired of listening to this sappy music? It's *so* old and . . . so BORING!"

"Kareem, watch it," said his father, waving a zucchini at him. "Sabah Fakhri is one of the greatest Syrian singers of all time. And this song is a love song to your city, to your country." His dad smiled at his mom, closed his eyes, and swayed to the music. Then he raised the zucchini in the air and serenaded her, completely off pitch.

The time gets longer and longer
I won't change and I won't waver
I miss you, oh, the light of my eyes.
I miss you, oh, the light of my eyes.

"Okay, okay. Mama, Baba. Please! You're killing me!" said Kareem. "Khalas, you win. Enough! I'm leaving, I'm leaving!"

"Actually, Kareem, hold on," said his dad, suddenly serious. He got up to turn off the music. "We need to talk to you."

"What's up?" asked Kareem. His mom and dad were now both looking at him intently. "Everything okay?"

"Kareem, where were you on Friday, when you said you were playing soccer?" his father asked.

Kareem froze. The hairs on the back of his neck stood up. *How'd they find out?*

"Kareem, I spoke to Adil's mom today," continued his mom. "You were not at the sports club on Friday. Adil went and nobody was there. Actually, it was closed—because of the protests."

Kareem's throat tightened, and he struggled to clear it. He searched for another excuse, but he knew there was no use.

"Tell the truth, ya Kareem. Do not lie to me." Her voice was sterner than he'd ever heard it.

Kareem looked at his feet. "I was at the protests."

His mom gave his dad a piercing *I told you* look.

"There were lots of young people, Mama," he said desperately. "It wasn't what you think. It was awesome. You . . . uh, it was . . . you should have . . ."

His tongue seemed to have turned to mush, and all the excitement brimming inside him was replaced with cold dread.

"Shiffit, iltilak . . . iltilak, ya Aziz!" his mom yelled. Her arms flailed and her voice rose with every word. "I told you he was there. I knew it. Your dad said you wouldn't do something like this, but I knew . . . I just . . ."

"Farah, please," said his dad, trying to calm her down. "Sit down. Let's talk about this."

Kareem clenched his fists, anger boiling in his chest. They should be proud. *He* was proud of what he and his friends—his *country*—had done on Friday.

"We had to go! We should *all* be going. You're being ridiculous!"

As soon as the words escaped him, he wished he could unsay them. He had already committed a major kid crime by disobeying his parents. And now, he'd talked back at them. *That*, by Syrian standards, was completely unacceptable.

His mom opened her mouth, but didn't say a word, wide-eyed with disbelief. His dad put his hand on her knee. Kareem suddenly wished she was still yelling.

"See, Aziz, what are we going to do with him?" his mom finally said. "Is this our son?"

"What if something happened," his dad said, "and we didn't even know you were there until you showed up on a gurney during our hospital shift?"

"It wasn't like that!" Kareem blurted. *Why did they always imagine the worst?* "It was peaceful."

"Habibi, alhamdulillah, it was peaceful *this time*," his mom said. "The government won't let this go on." She folded her arms over her head. "Habibi. We know what the protesters are doing is important, but you can't go by yourself. You're still so young. So naïve. Just look what this government did to the boys from Dara'a."

Kareem's cheeks flushed. He *wasn't* naïve. He'd known going was dangerous, but they had the numbers on their side. It was naïve to think things could stay as they were. It was time for change. That's what Ramy said. Kareem's parents had been silent for decades, and look where that had gotten them. They were scared and helpless.

"That's why we have to be out there!" Kareem's voice rose, even though he knew better than to yell at his parents. "*Because* of what happened to those boys."

His dad softly said, "You shouldn't be protesting without an adult."

"We had Ramy."

Kareem's mom shook her head. They sat in silence until she said, almost in tears: "Kareem, you are my only son."

He dropped his gaze again so as not to see the anguish in her face, but he couldn't unhear her voice. For the first time, he was completely at odds with his parents. This wasn't about going to a friend's house or asking for extra dessert. He didn't know how to make them understand.

"Mama, Baba, I'm sorry I upset you." His voice shook, just a little. The next words out of his mouth would bring on all their wrath. But he couldn't hold it in. "But I don't regret it. I had to go. And I'll do it again."

His dad jumped up.

"Listen to me, Kareem," he said in a voice Kareem had never heard before. "You cannot do this again. No—you *will not* do this again. I am warning you. If you do, there will be serious consequences." He paused for a moment before continuing. "You'll come home right after school every day, with no exceptions. I'm being very clear, Kareem. No more protests. Do you understand?"

Kareem stood silently in front of his parents. He didn't want to say yes. If he agreed, if he said what they wanted to hear, he would just be setting himself up to lie again. He was a part of this revolution; he wasn't going to shut himself up in his room. But they would never allow it. He had no choice but to lie to them.

"I can't hear you," said his father.

"Yes, Baba," Kareem said stiffly.

"Okay, get ready for dinner," his dad said. "Quickly, yalla."

Kareem ran to his room and flung himself down on his bed. He hated upsetting his parents, nearly making his mom cry, but he was right. He knew he was. They always imagined the worst because of what they saw at the hospital. But how could they tell him it was dangerous when they hadn't even been there? Children younger than Kareem had been in the crowd. Every family had to get out and stand together.

They ate dinner in silence. Afterward, Kareem excused himself to finish his homework but instead sketched the protest signs he had seen, continuing late into the night, even after his parents went to bed. He couldn't stop thinking about the chants and the people; how he'd marched arm-in-arm with his best friends. There had been so much hope, and an energy he could barely contain. He remembered the abandoned building—it really was the perfect spot for their next piece. They had to create something amazing, something to make people feel the way he'd felt earlier. Like change was coming.

He sketched birds in various positions, their wings stretched against the cloudy horizon, a rainbow in the background. But they'd already done birds.

"Houriyeh," he repeated over and over. It needed to be something simple yet big, something that they could finish in under five minutes.

He started drawing again. This time, chains. *Breaking* chains. Houriyeh Al'an. He could write it underneath in English, too— Freedom Now. #WeAreAllHamza. Kareem thought about his new curfew, the way his parents had reacted. He needed to do it now, while everybody was asleep. His parents had left him no other choice. He waited until he was sure they were fast asleep, and then texted Hassan.

Kareem

Yalla, get up. It's time to study.

Hassan

Now? It's the middle of the night. Tomorrow.

Kareem

UP. Come on. Now. We have a big test.

Kareem crouched on the balcony and tapped on Hassan's bedroom window. His heart pounded. *Come on, Hassan.* He'd never dreamed of sneaking out of his house at night before. His parents weren't strict, and he wasn't rebellious. So long as he told them where he was going, they rarely said no.

Hassan slid open his balcony's glass door and rubbed his eyes. "Kareem, what time is it? The adhan hasn't even blared. It must be like four a.m."

Kareem paused—he hadn't heard the morning call to prayer. It was definitely earlier than four. "Yalla, get dressed. I have a new piece for us."

"Are you kidding me?"

Kareem pulled the black sketchbook from his backpack and opened it to the broken chains. "We're going to paint this on that abandoned building, but we have to move fast. If we leave now, we'll be done before anybody wakes up."

Hassan grabbed Kareem's arm. "Why *now*? We have to plan. What about Yusuf? And George?"

"No, my parents found out we went to the protest, and they won't let me hang out after school anymore." Kareem pulled his arm free. "We have to do this now."

Hassan shook his head. "Habibi, I love the new piece, but if we get caught, you know what will happen to us."

Kareem did know. But he couldn't wait.

"Fine, I'll do it by myself. I don't need you."

Hassan flinched. A wave of guilt hit Kareem. He knew Hassan would never leave him to do something like this alone.

"Please, *please*, let's wait for morning and plan properly," begged Hassan. "We don't even have an escape plan. If we rush this, we'll get caught." Sweat beaded on his forehead. He looked scared. Kareem realized he was scared, too. But what if he never felt like this again? What if it all stopped? He'd been running on adrenaline since the protest. But now, standing on Hassan's balcony in the middle of the night with

TAGGING FREEDOM

a backpack full of spray cans, something in Kareem's body finally let go.

"Fine," he said, a lump forming in his throat. "Tomorrow. You promise?"

"I promise. Ma rah itrikak, habibi. Neither will Yusuf or George. I won't leave you. We're all in this together."

CHAPTER 6

SAMIRA

Sam stepped out into the fresh spring air, pulled the door shut behind her, and skipped down the back stairs and around to the main road. She had barely slept in anticipation of the big game and banner reveal. Plus, this was her first official Spirit Squad event.

"Hey, what took you so long?" Ellie said, from Sam's front step. It was their usual meeting spot. "The game already started! Let me guess. Five tries to get that outfit right."

"Four," Sam said, placing her hands on her hips. "Ha-ha. Okay, Miss Know-It-All. If you know me so well, what am I thinking?"

"What an *amazing* best friend you have," said Ellie, beaming. "And how you missed me so much."

"Right," said Sam, laughing. "That's exactly what I was thinking."

"Oh, and how you should listen to me more often, because I'm so wise," said Ellie. "And you're probably thinking about chocolate chip cookies, too. Doesn't everybody, on some level, always think about chocolate chip cookies?"

Sam rolled her eyes and started walking, suddenly annoyed all over again.

I should listen to her more often? OMG. That's how she's starting our conversation, after two days of not speaking? After what happened on Friday?

"Hey, wait up, why are you walking so fast?" Ellie said, running to catch up. Ellie was wearing her usual: blue jeans, a faded yellow tie-dyed T-shirt, and her sparkly silver Converse. Her untied laces flapped against the sidewalk with every step.

Sam stuffed her hands in her pockets and took a deep breath.

I just need to tell her how I felt on Friday. Be honest. Talk it out.

"So, do you want to help make posters for the food pantry's spring fair?" Ellie asked as they made their way down the block.

Sam stopped abruptly and turned to Ellie.

"Are you kidding me?" Sam's face grew hot.

"What?" Ellie looked confused.

"Ellie, I'm really upset about what happened Friday. You're my best friend and I really needed you. I mean . . ." Sam paused.

I shouldn't have to explain this.

"You *knew* how nervous I'd be at that meeting, alone," she continued. "I begged you to come with me. And you just left me. I would have never made you go by yourself."

Ellie sighed and crossed her arms. "Maybe you've blocked out what Cat did to you before, but I can't. I'm not going to sit around and watch it happen again."

"I'm not joining for Cat," Sam shot back. "Spirit Squad is not only about Cat. It's so perfect for me. Why can't you trust *me*?"

"Oh, come on, Sam," said Ellie. "Spirit Squad will always be about Cat. She rules that group."

Sam walked the rest of the block in silence. She knew Ellie was probably right about Cat. But that wasn't the point. They rounded the corner to the school's field.

"Don't you get it, Eleanora Gold?" Sam said. "It's not about whether Cat's in charge or not. It's about standing next to your BFF. I was so nervous, I thought I was going to puke. And you didn't care. Plus, I always help you with your posters. Have you ever asked for help and I said no? Never."

"Sam, if you're that nervous, it's a sign that there's something wrong—with Cat, with Spirit Squad, with all of it. They're just . . . so fake," Ellie said. "Plus, a banner for Spirit Squad is not the same as posters for the food pantry. Mine's for a worthy cause, not some stupid game."

Sam threw her hands up in the air and walked away.

"Hey, where are you going?" Ellie hurried to catch up. "We're talking."

"No, *you're* talking. You're not listening to me at all; you're just doing the same thing you always do."

"Which is what?" said Ellie, her eyes narrowing.

"Being judgy." Sam placed her hands on her hips and flared her nostrils. "Why is it that the food pantry is a worthy cause and Spirit Squad is terrible? And why do you always want to think about sad things, anyway? You know, it's okay to have fun, Ellie. We don't have to save the world. We're just kids."

"Sam! Sam! Over here!" Lucy was waving from the gym's entrance. "Come on, we're going to be late!"

"Oh, look, my 'fake' friends are waiting for me," Sam said. "I have to go. It's time for me to get *used*."

"Okay, Sam, be that way. I'm just trying to protect you." Ellie stalked away.

Protect me?! Sam wanted to explode. She headed to the gym, trying to calm herself down. This was not how she wanted her banner reveal day to begin. She forced a big smile and followed Lucy into the gym's bathroom, where Avery and Cat were in front of the mirror, applying shiny pink lip gloss.

"Look who I found outside," said Lucy, smiling.

"Hi, Sam," said Avery. "Ready for the big game?"

Sam nodded, struggling to shake off the conversation with Ellie. She wanted to be excited, not silently fuming.

"Okay, everybody grab a bag, and let's get out there." Cat slipped the gloss into her back pocket and grabbed a bag of Spirit Squad equipment.

Sam checked her hair in the mirror and took off her jean jacket to reveal a glittery tank top that peeked out from beneath her jumper. She had layered it perfectly. She was normally a jeans and T-shirt kinda girl, but today was special.

"Oooh, I love your jumper and tank top combo," said Avery. "Super cute."

"Thanks!"

Not school appropriate, her father would say. And Sam had avoided taking off her jacket in front of Ellie. She didn't want to discuss her outfit—it was just a piece of clothing. Her parents didn't get that it was what most kids wore at school.

Sam flipped her long, curly hair around her shoulders and suddenly wished she'd snuck some lip gloss, too. When she turned, she found Cat staring at her.

"How are your eyelashes so long?" Cat asked. "Are you related to a llama or something?"

"I know, aren't they beautiful?" Lucy said. "And her hair. I think she has the most beautiful hair in the entire school!"

Sam turned bright red at the attention.

"But she should wear it up. It'll look better." Cat looked at Avery and Lucy. "Don't you think?"

"I guess," said Lucy. "Sam, your hair looks great however you wear it."

"Thanks, Lucy," mumbled Sam. She twirled her hair into a high bun, leaving a few strands to cascade down. She'd always thought her hair looked best natural, hanging below her shoulders, but she didn't want to argue. "How's this?"

"Perfect!" Cat swung her own shiny hair around. "Let's go."

Sam shrugged and grabbed a garbage bag of noisemakers. She followed the others out to the field, where the game was already in full swing. They climbed into the third row of stands. Sam's banner hung high above the home team's bench, and a surge of pride ran through her. She'd done it practically by herself, and it was amazing. The letters popped, just as she had imagined. Fierce, but still a little playful. And her lion was pretty good, given that was usually Ellie's job. For a moment, she wished her parents could see it.

"It looks so good!" Lucy cried.

Sam grinned.

On the field, AMS had control of the ball. Sam took a seat next to Lucy, who had plopped her bag of signs at her feet. "One to nothing already? We're totally gonna win."

"I know," said Lucy. "The way Dylan and Amari pass to each other. They're awesome!"

Sam searched for Dylan in his blue and gold jersey. She found Amari first, with his dark, high Afro and the name LIGHT on the back of his jersey. He had the ball at midfield but soon passed it to the tall, blond boy with SPENCER on his jersey, who flew down the right-hand side of the field. She sighed. Dylan was so cute. And *fast*.

Without warning, a pair of purple plastic pom-poms hit her head.

"Catch," said Cat, as she and Avery launched more pom-poms into the crowd.

Sam forced a smile. "Pom-pom attack. Hate when that happens."

Lucy rolled her eyes toward Cat, so only Sam could see, then shrugged and grinned. Sam grinned back.

"Let's go, squad," yelled Cat. "In formation."

The Spirit Squad ran to the front and stood in teams of two, with Cat and Tom, each carrying bullhorns, flanked by Avery and James on one side and Lucy on the other.

"Come on." Lucy waved to Sam. "Get down here!"

Sam's stomach fluttered. She didn't mind performances, usually, but this was different. Now she was about to go in front of the whole school with Cat Spencer. For so long, she had *not* been welcome, and now she was being beckoned to join, for everyone to see. She bit her lip and took in a deep breath.

"Come on, Sam," Lucy yelled again. "Come on!"

Sam ran up to the front and stood slightly behind Lucy. She looked up at the sea of pom-poms and timidly waved her own. Cat and Tom led the crowd in a call-and-response cheer by grade. As Cat finished sixth grade, and Tom started with the seventh, the tension in Sam's back and shoulders began to loosen. This wasn't so bad. They were just cheering, and she definitely knew how to do that. Sam loved happy, festive moments. She thrust her pom-poms in the air, letting the crowd's cheers and happy faces propel her arms upward.

Then she spotted Ellie sitting with the Art Club at the top of the bleachers. She wasn't cheering or talking to anyone. She just sat there. The chants flattened around Sam like a tire slowly emptying of air.

She should be excited for me. She should be admiring my banner and standing by my side.

Sam punched her clenched fists back into the air as Cat led the school in an "AMS, We're #1" cheer.

A roar went up. Sam turned and saw Dylan jump on Amari in celebration of another goal.

The crowd chanted Amari's name. Cheers and yells and screams filled the next hour as Amari and Dylan traded turns scoring goals. The Spirit Squad burst into a round of "Here we go, Allansdale, here we go!" *clap clap*, bringing the AMS fans to their feet.

Sam cheered and kicked and pom-pomed. Occasionally, she sensed eyes boring through her, but whenever she looked at Ellie, Ellie wasn't looking back.

Toward the end of the game, Sam noticed Ellie had left, and for a brief moment, her heart dropped. Ellie knew how hard the last few years had been for Sam. How could she be angry now that Sam was finally being invited in and accepted? Caught up in the next cheer, though, she began to feel lighter—as if a smothering, sloth-like creature had hopped off her shoulders. She hated to admit it, but now that Ellie wasn't watching, Sam could finally breathe.

"Final score," the referee yelled. "AMS, four; Evergreen Prep, one."

The players lined up to shake hands, while the cheering crowd began to disperse.

"Okay, Spirit Squad, let's clean this place up." Cat handed out garbage bags but left the others to do the work while she fielded compliments from parents at the bottom of the bleachers.

Sam picked up wrappers and streamers, and watched Amari and Dylan make their way over to the stands from the corner of her eye.

"Hey, sis," Dylan called to Cat. "Did you see my last shot? Awesome, right?"

"Don't get too into yourself, bro." Cat crossed her arms. "It's just soccer."

"Whoa, whoa, whoa!" Amari dropped his soccer kit and held up his hands. "Don't dis the game, people. Don't dis the game."

Cat laughed, her expression changing. "I didn't mean it like that! You know we have to keep Dylan's ego in check."

"Okay," Amari grinned. "I'm fine with dissing the playa." He held out a fist for Cat to awkwardly bump.

Looking at Cat's face, it suddenly dawned on Sam—Cat liked Amari! This was the first time she'd seen Cat be less than perfect, and for a split second, she thought she might have seen the real Cat. In that moment, Cat's sharp angles almost softened to something more curved and vulnerable.

Almost.

"Sam! Can you help clear the trash? That's part of what we do in Spirit Squad."

"That's what I'm doing," said Sam, startled, but Cat had already turned away.

"Hey, Sam," said Dylan, making eye contact and smiling wide. "What did you think of the game?"

"It was awesome!" *A little too eager, Sam? Come on, play it cool.* She flushed and tried to think of things that made her laugh. She'd read an article that said laughter could stop you from blushing. Then again, so would avoiding your crush. "You . . . you guys were totally amazing out there."

"Yes . . . I . . . was!" Amari said with a big, theatrical dab. He suavely moved his hand from across his chest, through his Afro, and flashed his big, dark eyes at them.

Sam couldn't help laughing.

"Okay, Mr. Modest," she teased. "That's your new nickname, by the way."

"Why should I be modest when I'm this good!" He bumped a soccer ball on alternating knees and then grabbed the ball out of midair. "Hat trick good!"

"That was legit," said Cat, moving closer to Amari. "Three goals is amazing."

Amari grinned, but at Sam. "See?"

"Oh, please. I've known you since you were in kindergarten, Amari Light," said Sam, waving him away. "I knew you when Alexis made fun of your teddy bear and you cried for two days about it."

Dylan laughed and bumped against Amari. "Ha, you cried because of a teddy bear!"

"Don't you dare make fun of Babou like that, you heartless people," Amari said, puffing up his chest. "He's still my best friend."

"That seems about right," said Sam. She glanced at Cat, but Cat seemed decidedly unamused. Sam never understood what made Cat happy or upset, but she'd definitely turned sour now.

"Sam, you're coming to our party next week, right?" Dylan asked.

Sam's heart pounded. He was asking her, in front of everyone, to go to his party. She suddenly forgot how to speak English.

"I mean, I—I didn't . . . ," she stammered. "Uh, what party?"

"Cat." Dylan side-eyed his sister. "You said you asked the whole Spirit Squad."

"Oh, yeah. I just didn't get a chance to tell Sam yet. Chill out, bro. It's no big deal."

"Well, you should come," said Dylan to Sam. "It'll be fun."

Sam smiled, not sure where to look. "Yeah, I'll be there."

"We gotta go!" Amari interrupted, pulling on Dylan's jersey. "We're going to be late. Coach will want to congratulate his star player." He pointed at his chest and gave an exaggerated wink. "That's me."

"Okay, Mr. Modest." Sam rolled her eyes, laughing again. Amari always made her laugh.

Amari and Dylan walked off, punching each other and jumping around like big, playful puppies. Sam could hardly believe it. Dylan Spencer just invited *her* to a party!

"Get back to work, Sam," Cat barked. She shoved another bag toward Sam, even though her garbage bag was barely full. "We don't have all day."

Sam went back to picking up trash, wondering what had changed Cat's mood. Lucy came up behind her and said, with a backward glance at Amari and Dylan: "A personal invitation, huh?"

They both giggled.

When they'd finished clearing up the trash, Lucy said, "Want to walk home with me?"

Sam nodded, beaming. Her banner had been a hit, she couldn't remember ever having this much fun at school, Dylan Spencer invited her to a party, and now she was walking home with a new friend.

She still wished Ellie could see her right now. If she wasn't so stubborn and judgy, they could all be walking home together, having a great time. Sam pushed away those thoughts. She wasn't going to let Eleanora Gold ruin her perfect moment.

Sam and Lucy chatted all the way home, talking about the game and Dylan's party. As they walked up Sam's street, Sam glanced across at Ellie's house. Her bedroom windows were shuttered. Since they were kids, that had been her signal that she was upset. It was official—they were definitely in a fight.

CHAPTER 7

KAREEM

Kareem sprayed the final silver link and whispered, "The chain's done on this side."

"Almost done here, too," replied Yusuf.

"Yalla, finish up." Hassan was at the corner of the building. "We're a minute over."

The chain spanned the abandoned building's entire wall. At its center, Kareem had painted a single, broken link with bits of metal flying off it. They'd wanted to have cuffed arms ripping the chains apart, but it was too difficult to paint quickly. Above the broken chain, Hassan had written "Houriyeh" in large red letters. Underneath, Yusuf had added "Al'an."

Hassan, Yusuf, and George had spent Saturday convincing Kareem they needed a proper escape plan. Hassan made the case for waiting until Friday morning—that way, they could paint their newest graffiti while sermons blared from the city's minarets and everyone was inside praying. The shops would be shuttered, and the streets abandoned. With Damascus practically a ghost town, they'd have at least twenty minutes to complete the piece before mosque-goers either headed home or went out to start more protests.

The only thing the boys couldn't agree on was whether to tag it #WeAreAllHamza. Kareem and Yusuf wanted to, but Ramy was dead set against the idea.

Kareem stepped back to admire their finished piece. "Let's do it." He lifted the black spray can above his head and aimed next to "Al'an." His fingers tingled, and his heart pounded harder as adrenaline pumped through him. "Let's add the hashtag, guys. Come on. Please!"

Just as he pressed down on the nozzle, Ramy appeared from around the corner, frantically shouting, "Go, go! Shabiha. They're here!"

Three young men dressed in black were close on Ramy's heels. "Khawana, khawana!"

"Traitors?" Kareem yelled back. "For real?"

He dropped his can and took off due east, toward the old, walled part of the city. The others fanned out, just like they had planned. Yusuf bolted west toward the bridge; George north, toward the school; and Hassan south, toward the train station.

Kareem's heart felt like it might leap from his chest. Ramy had given them pointers on what to do if this happened—sprint, take random turns, and head into big crowds if possible. But the reality of being chased was so different from how he'd imagined it. Kareem hoped the shabiha would chase after him or Yusuf or George—any of them except Hassan. Hassan wasn't fast; he was usually the last chosen for sports teams. The rest of them would have a better shot at outrunning these thugs.

He glanced over his shoulder. A bald man with a beard, dressed in all black, was closing the distance between them.

The shabiha.

Ghosts. That's what people called the thugs hired by the government to intimidate and stop the protesters. This one seemed to float, shadowing Kareem's every move.

Kareem ran faster toward the old city. He knew every turn and hideout within its walls, which would give him a clear advantage. Unlike Hassan, Kareem could outrun almost anybody. He'd won every race since second grade. But worrying about Hassan slowed him down. It was like moving in slow motion, with flailing arms and barbells for feet.

He ran breathlessly down the large boulevard. His pounding heart made the sidewalk feel like it was quivering with each step. But as fast as Kareem was, the man behind him lost no ground. He was fast, too.

Come on, Kareem. Run smarter.

Remembering a shortcut he used to take to his grandmother's mosaic box shop in the old city, he made a sharp left down an alleyway that cut diagonally through the city, then took the side road toward the great mosque. From there, he zigzagged down other little alleys. In the distance, he could hear a hum of voices exiting the mosque.

Yes! Kareem thought. *They're done.*

As he cut through the last alley, a sea of faithful men emptied into the square. Kareem approached the crowd. He slowed to a fast gait until he reached the mosque's side entrance, where he threw his cap and jacket on top of the pile of shoes.

Men dispersed, eager to get to lunch. Kareem couldn't see his tail anymore. He joined a group, walking among them with his chin tucked down. At every turn, he slipped into a different group of men. He pulled out his phone to send his coded *I'm okay* message, then froze.

Their fingerprints would be on the spray cans.

He forced himself to send his message—

Kareem

Futbol today?

Two minutes passed.

Yusuf

I'm down.

Another minute.

George

Me too!

57

Kareem's panic rose as he stared at his phone. *Come on, Hassan.*

More minutes passed.

Kareem walked home in a daze. Why wasn't Hassan texting? *Yalla, habibi. Where's your message? Come on.*

◊

By the time Kareem reached his apartment building an hour later, there was still no word from Hassan. He wanted to throw up. They always planned their escapes, but they'd never discussed what to do if someone was caught.

He wanted to call Yusuf or George, but they had a pact—no calls until everybody was safe. They couldn't chance the mukhabarat finding the others through their phones.

Please, please, please let Hassan be sitting on my couch.

He opened the front door. Hassan wasn't there. Kareem's parents were in the dining room, preparing the table for lunch. Kareem stood in the doorway and clutched his phone.

"Habibi, yalla, grab a chair." His mom glanced at him and put down her bowl of warm pita bread. "Why do you look like that? What's wrong?"

Come on, Hassan, come on.

Kareem didn't know what to do. Should he tell them? They'd be furious—they thought he'd gone over to Hassan's to help with a school project. But if something had happened to

Hassan, his parents needed to know. They would tell Hassan's parents so Hassan's parents could try to get him out.

"Kareem, what's wrong?" urged his mom. "You look like you've seen a ghost."

Kareem braced himself. "Mama. Baba." It was hard to speak. "I think . . . I think the mukhabarat . . . I think they got him." His voice cracked. Tears filled his eyes and streamed down his face.

"Who, habibi?" His mom's voice rose as she came closer. "They got who?"

"He hasn't texted."

"Who do they have?" his dad asked firmly.

"Hassan." Sobbing, Kareem slumped to the floor. "He's supposed to text, but he hasn't."

"Why would the mukhabarat want Hassan? What text?"

Kareem could barely see his parents through his tears.

"Why do you have paint on your clothes? On your hands?" His father looked straight into his eyes. "What were you doing that the mukhabarat would have Hassan?"

Pausing to swallow his tears, Kareem haltingly explained. "We were graffitiing the old, abandoned building on Shara'a al-Thawra."

"Graffitiing?" yelled his father. "Didn't we just have this conversation? What is wrong with you?"

Kareem tensed. His best friend had probably been arrested, and it was all his fault.

His father turned away and took a deep breath. When he turned back to face Kareem, his expression was stern, but he seemed slightly calmer. "Okay, tell me everything."

As Kareem told the full story, his dad paced the room, his face growing progressively redder. His mom sat motionless at the table.

"We have to go to Hassan's house," his dad said to his mom when Kareem finally finished.

Kareem lowered his eyes and noticed red paint on his shoes. His phone vibrated.

Hassan

I'm in!

"He's okay! He's okay!" Kareem jumped up and held out his phone. "He just texted! Hassan's okay." He flopped backward onto a chair and practically sang, "He's okay! He's okay!"

"What do you think you're doing, Kareem?" his dad cried. "Do you think this is a game? You got lucky this time, but we don't know if you're in the clear yet. They could still come after you." He paused. "Did they see you?"

Kareem nodded. And there were spray cans with their fingerprints. They weren't out of this yet. He looked at his parents, who were staring at each other intently. With a single eyebrow lift from his dad, Kareem knew an unspoken conversation had just taken place between them.

"What?" Kareem looked suspiciously at them. "What's happening?"

His mom nodded at his dad, and Kareem realized that something important had been decided.

"Kareem, go to your room," his father said. "Now."

◊

Kareem pressed his ear to his bedroom wall but couldn't make out his parents' hushed words.

Between the chase and worrying about Hassan, he'd never been so scared in his life. He replayed the morning in his head. Everything had gone to plan—they'd sprayed quickly, finished before the call to prayer, and separated like they were supposed to in an emergency. In the end, they'd even outrun the mukhabarat. It was a close call, but overall, a success.

Still—it might not be over. Would the mukhabarat figure out who they were? And what were his *parents* going to do?

Kareem fell back onto his bed and texted Hassan.

Kareem

How are you feeling? Everything okay?

Hassan

Yeah, I'm okay. Tired.

Kareem

Might not be able to study anymore. I think I'm
in trouble.

Hassan

Kareem

Oh, and my parents might call your parents.

Hassan

Kareem put his phone away and tried listening at the door again. It sounded like his parents were already making a call. Surely it was too dangerous to discuss this with Hassan's parents by phone. But who else could they be talking to?

An hour later, they called him into the living room. His mother sat on a fancy, gold settee in the corner. His father stood behind her, resting his hands on the chair's curved backrest.

"Kareem," he said solemnly. "We have been considering something for some time, and today confirms it's what we must do."

Kareem stiffened like he was waiting to be sentenced in front of a judge. He'd already thought through some potential punishments they might dole out. Would they keep him home until the protests were over? Escort him to and from school?

"We just spoke to my brother," his mother continued. "We're sending you to live with his family."

Kareem just stood there. He couldn't take it in. He must have misheard.

"When you arrive, you might have to apply for asylum. But we have a year left on our visitors' visa, so we don't have to decide that right away."

Kareem shook his head. This wasn't a scenario he'd ever imagined.

"Mama, Baba, what are you talking about?"

"You heard us," his father said calmly. "You're going to live with Khalo Ahmed in America."

CHAPTER 8

Samira

Sam paced outside the kitchen, eavesdropping on her parents.

"Farah, do not worry," her dad said into the phone. "I sent you the e-ticket. I promise I'll take good care of him."

Ever since her parents agreed to her cousin Kareem coming to live with them, the household had been in a frenzy. Her mom had spent the last two days turning the basement into a bedroom, and her dad had been working on enrolling Kareem in school.

In all the excitement, Sam hadn't found the right moment to ask about the party. Of course, she wasn't going to say it was *Dylan's* party. She'd say she was going to Ellie's house; that way there wouldn't be any questions. Parties with boys were *definitely* on the NO list.

Sam put a light sweater on over her summer dress, primped her curls in the mirror, and picked up her backpack. She was already a half hour late.

"Mom, Dad, I'm going to Ellie's house."

"We're having dinner at six, habibti," her mom called. "Don't be late."

"I won't."

Tingling with excitement, Sam grabbed her bike from the garage but left the helmet on a utility shelf.

Cat's house is only a few blocks. That thing will totally ruin my hair.

She coasted down the driveway, glancing at Ellie's window across the street. It was still shuttered. She knew she shouldn't use Ellie as an excuse when they hadn't spoken since the soccer game. But she was definitely not going to apologize first. It wasn't fair for Ellie to make her choose between Spirit Squad and her best friend. Best friends didn't do that. This time, Ellie needed to understand that her judgy-ness was the real problem.

The weight of the last few days flew off Sam as she pedaled fast and the wind played with her curls. What would she say to Dylan? One of the most popular boys in school had invited her to his party. What if he liked her? After all, he hadn't invited a whole bunch of people at once—he'd singled her out. But maybe he was just really friendly. Either way, whenever she was around him, she could barely put two words together.

But what could she do if he *did* like her? It wasn't like she could openly be his girlfriend. Before she could even walk, her parents had hammered home that girlfriends and boyfriends weren't allowed in their culture. That was for after she'd finished college, when she was more mature and ready to settle down. Even then, they wouldn't approve of a "boyfriend." They would say she was "talking to" or "getting to know" a boy. Her parents called it halal dating: dating for the purpose of marrying. Halal dating was definitely not allowed in middle school.

Sam wondered whether Kareem had a girlfriend in Syria. Or if he liked someone? Maybe kids over there couldn't date, but surely they had crushes. She hadn't seen Kareem in five years, since they took a family trip to Disney World together. She remembered him as fun and silly, always playing practical jokes.

She loved the idea of having her cousin at school. He was the closest thing she had to a real sibling, even though they didn't talk much because of the distance. Maybe they could speak in Arabic when they didn't want others to understand.

Sam's curls blew over her eyes, and she wished she'd worn her helmet. Helmet head was better than Hairzilla. She turned into the Spencers' driveway and took in the peaked brick house, the perfectly manicured lawn, and the enormous trees that canopied the driveway.

Sam rested her bike against the garage door and headed through an ornate black gate. Kids' voices came from the backyard. She'd hoped to sneak into the bathroom to fix her hair and put on lip gloss before anybody saw her, but Dylan suddenly appeared from nowhere. Her mouth went dry.

"Hey, Sam." He opened another gate and ushered her through to a pool area. "You made it!"

Sam flushed.

Inside, a dozen AMS seventh and eighth graders were gathered around the pool and barbecue, laughing and eating. Some were even in swimsuits. The smell of hot dogs and hamburgers filled the air.

"I can't believe people are swimming!" Sam said. "It's barely spring."

"Yeah, but the pool's heated. You should try it. It's prime!" Dylan pointed to her backpack. "Did you bring your swimsuit?"

"Oh . . . um . . . no," Sam mumbled.

Cat walked up behind her brother. "I totally forgot to tell her to bring one. Sorry, Sam." She took a sip of punch. "You can borrow one of my spare bikinis if you want."

Sam blushed. "Uh, thanks, I'm good. It's too cold, I think." She scanned the backyard and spotted Lucy and Avery playing Jenga with James and Alex. The others were all eighth graders she didn't know.

"Sam!" Lucy waved. "Over here!"

Cat headed for the table. Dylan started after her, but Cat pushed him away and snapped, "Why are you always following me around?"

"Why are you always so mean? I'm sick of it."

Awkward.

Sam hurriedly joined Lucy and the others, eager to get away from the siblings' bickering. She dropped into a spare seat, smiling around at the group.

"What happened to your hair?" asked Cat, catching up. Sam reached up to try to smooth her windswept curls.

Amari joined them and grabbed a handful of popcorn. "I like your hair like that, Sam."

Sam startled. "Thanks, Amari. I guess we both have wild hair today."

"What? My hair is fire!" Amari caressed his Afro and pouted. "Please *do not* insult my amazing hair again, thank you very much."

"Oh yeah, forgot about Mr. Modest over here." Sam chuckled. "My bad, my bad."

Amari grinned at her, then raced to the pool and cannonballed in, creating a tidal wave over the lounge chairs. Dylan followed him. They wrestled for a few minutes, then roped two other boys into a game of chicken. Sam laughed, watching them splash around on each other's shoulders.

"Oh my God, they're so immature," said Cat, unamused.

Lucy was intensely considering her next Jenga move. "I have to focus. The loser has to jump in the pool with their clothes on."

"Whoa," said Sam. "High stakes."

Lucy took her turn and exhaled when the tower held steady. "I'm so glad your parents let you come, Sam," she said.

"I sort of told them I was at Ellie's."

Cat smirked. "I'm surprised you didn't bring her along. You're usually inseparable."

"She's busy," Sam mumbled, stuffing some chips in her mouth. Ellie would never have come, even if she'd been invited.

"It would really help if she grew her hair out, you know," Cat said. "She's nice and all, but it's weird that she wants to look like a boy."

Sam shifted in her seat.

"She doesn't even wear shoes half the time. Whenever I see her outside of school, she's barefoot. What's up with that?"

"You know, she's just Ellie," Sam said, biting her lip.

"She sure is." Cat looked over at the pool. "Come on, Amari, get him! Bring him DOWN!" She took another sip of punch and considered Sam seriously. "You like my brother, don't you?"

Sam nearly choked on her chips. Her heart pounded. She was fairly sure her traitorous face had gone fire-engine red. Without saying a word, she was inadvertently telling the wrong person her deepest secret. She wished the floor would open and swallow her whole. Or at least that the Jenga tower would topple as a distraction.

"It's okay," Cat said, shrugging. "Half the girls at AMS have a crush on him. God knows why." She patted Sam's hand, stood, and started for the food table. "Don't worry, I won't tell him. Just stay away from Amari. He's mine."

"Oh, right," Sam mumbled. "Totally not interested in Amari."

Sam watched Cat chat easily with a group of eighth graders, commanding the space like usual. She might be the younger sister, but she was definitely the one in charge. Her letters were even edgier than Sam had previously thought. Piercing, icicle-like.

Much like the cold water that sprinkled down on Sam's shoulders.

"Ahh!" she screamed.

Dylan was behind her, grinning. "I'm so sorry, did I get you wet?"

"You did it on purpose!" She smiled up at him.

"No," said Amari. "On purpose would look like this." He pulled out a water gun, squirted each of the girls, and ran away.

Dylan laughed and pulled out his own weapon.

"Let's go!" yelled Avery. "Water fight!"

Sam's phone vibrated, but she ignored it. She grabbed two soakers from a box of pool toys and filled them with water. Over the next half hour, they jumped, hid, ducked, rolled, sprayed, and doused each other. Every time she paused for a moment, she found either Amari or Dylan aiming at her. They were everywhere.

"You can't hide from me!" Amari called.

Sam giggled and took cover behind some potted plants. Her phone vibrated over and over in her back pocket. She checked to make sure she was in the clear and pulled it out.

Five missed calls from her parents. A bunch of unread messages, all from Ellie.

Oh no.

Ellie

Your parents were here.

Ellie

They're mad.

Ellie

I'm not sure what you told them.

Ellie

You're probably with your new "friends."

Ellie

You need to get home.

Ellie

Now.

Ellie

Your dad looked so mad!

"Shoot. Shoot. Shoot," Sam mumbled to herself as she grabbed her stuff and ran for the back gate.

"Hey, where you going?" Dylan caught up right as Sam jumped on her bike. Amari was close behind.

"I have to go," she said, breathless. "I'm sorry."

Amari smiled. "Did we scare you off?"

"You wish."

Sam rode home as fast as she could. This was bad. There was no good way to explain why she hadn't been at Ellie's like she'd said, or why she was soaking wet. She'd have to admit she lied. Why did they have to walk over to Ellie's to get her? Most parents would just call, but her dad took any opportunity to chat with Sheriff Gold—he thought Americans were too closed off from their neighbors. He loved randomly knocking on people's doors to say hi. Why couldn't Sam's parents be regular, leave-me-alone, please-don't-come-by-unless-you-call-first Americans?

They were waiting for her in the foyer.

"I'm sorry, Baba, Mama," said Sam. "I went to Cat's house to meet some friends."

Her mom crossed her arms. "You lied! And Cat? Isn't she the one who—"

"You were busy, Mama." Sam didn't want her parents to remember Cat. "I didn't think it mattered whether I was at Ellie's or Cat's. I mean, I *was* going to Ellie's, but then Cat called. We were just hanging out."

"And why are you all wet?" her dad asked.

"There was a water fight. We were playing, and I didn't hear your calls."

Sam's mom shook her head in disapproval and her dad frowned. They stood in silence, while her dad paced around the room.

"Samira Sukkari, if you have to lie to us, then there's a problem with your friends," said her dad. "This is totally unacceptable. You're grounded until further notice. Go to your room."

"Yes, Baba. Yes, Mama." Sam paused in the doorway. "I'm sorry I lied to you."

Sam ran upstairs, flopped onto her bed, and groaned. This was totally unfair. Her friends never had to lie because their parents weren't this strict. And now she was grounded for God knows how long.

As she peeled off her damp socks and sweater, she thought about the party and the water fight. She smiled. She'd had a blast. It was totally worth it. And maybe she was imagining things, but it felt like Dylan had noticed her all afternoon. Of course, there was still the Cat problem. She knew Cat couldn't be trusted with her secret. Figuring out how to manage her—with her sharp, protruding, nosy letters—wasn't going to be easy.

She looked across the street at Ellie's shuttered window again.

Ellie was obviously still mad at her. But at least she had tried to warn Sam. She picked up her phone. She needed to say something.

Sam

I know you're still mad. TBH I'm still mad too.

Sam

But thank you for the warnings.

Ellie

You're welcome.

Ellie

But . . . told you that crowd is trouble.

Sam chucked her phone onto her pillows. *Eleanora Gold, arrgh. Why? Why are you like this?*

CHAPTER 9

KAREEM

Kareem gazed out the window as they took off over the Mediterranean. The sea below sparkled in the spring sun and Beirut slowly disappeared as they climbed into the clouds.

He rubbed his red, swollen eyes. He'd done everything to try to convince his parents not to send him away, but nothing had worked. They'd given him two days to pack and say goodbye to his friends; then his father had driven him to Beirut, where they'd spent two nights at a cousin's house. At the airport that morning, Kareem had broken down in tears outside the security line. He had never been so angry.

He opened his sketchbook on his lap. His father had told him to leave it behind, that they couldn't afford to have the soldiers on the Lebanese-Syrian border find it in his backpack. But Kareem hadn't listened. He needed his sketchbook. A few days ago, he'd been spray-painting chains on a building. Now, he was on his way to a country where most people couldn't even find Syria on a map.

He flipped through his sketches, remembering how he, Hassan, Yusuf, and George had discussed each of them individually. They had debated how long each piece would take, their locations, which words they would include. His throat tightened. How could he abandon his friends during the most important event to happen to their country in decades? His parents had reassured him that he could return once things had calmed down, but Kareem knew deep down that wouldn't happen anytime soon. People were angry, and the bottle had been uncorked. There was no pushing everybody back inside. A revolution was erupting, and he was heading to America, a country that didn't care. At least, that's what he'd heard.

Kareem flipped to a clean page and started drawing. He thought about how he and Hassan had said goodbye to each other in his living room, the night before he left for Beirut. He couldn't even look at his best friend without choking up.

Hassan had finally broken the silence.

"Habibi, it won't be for long," he said. "You'll be back before you know it. It's like a vacation. Like . . . like you're going to Disneyland."

Kareem didn't know what to say. His eyes were full of tears. Hassan came over and put his arms around him.

"You have to get a picture with Mickey, okay?" he said, squeezing him tight. "And Goofy. It will be like looking in the mirror."

Kareem pulled back in disbelief, then cracked up.

"Ana Goofy?!" he said, laughing, because it was better than crying. "Inta Goofy. You are Goofy and Mickey and Minnie all in one."

"Is that any way to speak to your elders?" Hassan pretended to turn serious. "Ihtiram halak. Watch it, young man. I'm two years older."

Kareem tackled Hassan, trying to make him beg for mercy. They laughed and laughed until Kareem's father came in and said it was time to go.

Hurtling through the sky, farther from home by the second, Kareem drew a bird with no wings walking on a tree that lay on a dark road, its roots exposed. And then he fell asleep, his sketchbook still open, his pencil falling from his hand.

CHAPTER 10

SAMĪRA

Samira's week had been a disaster. After grounding her on Saturday, her father didn't even let her go to the Islamic Center on Sunday. Instead, he spent the entire morning lecturing her about trust and integrity. Sam had spent the rest of the week trying to make it up to them. She made her bed, did the dishes without being asked, tidied the living room every afternoon, and did whatever she was told, without a single complaint.

Tonight, finally, she had something to be excited about—Kareem was arriving. She couldn't wait to see her cousin again. Plus, she hoped her parents would start focusing on him, instead of her bad behavior.

Sam threw her backpack on the dining room table and headed into the kitchen.

"OMG, it's hot in here." She timidly gave her mom a kiss on the cheek. "And it smells *so* good."

Her mom's side-eye suggested she was unimpressed by Sam's compliments. Sam's father had delivered the lectures and doled out the punishment, but, in some ways, her mom's silence was worse.

Sam peeked inside a pot filled with stuffed grape leaves, each the size of a tiny sausage, neatly piled in concentric circles. Then she checked the oven, where a big bubble of puff pastry was browning like a beautiful pillow. To the right of the stove stood a bowl of finely chopped parsley, tomatoes, onions, and burghul, still unmixed.

"Mmmm . . . fatayer, warak 'anab, and tabbouleh. This looks awesome."

Sam's mom nodded and kept stirring the pot.

"You made shishbarak!" Sam salivated at the quarter-sized dumplings floating in yogurt stew. It was her favorite dish of all time, and something her mom only made on special occasions. "I can't remember the last time you made this, Mama."

"Samira, coming to the US alone at thirteen isn't easy," said her mom, stirring intently. If she stopped, the whole dish would be ruined. "I want Kareem to feel at home and welcomed." She finally looked at Sam, her eyes serious. "I expect you to help him as much as you can."

Sam nodded. "Of course, Mama."

Her mom removed the large pot from the stove. "Kareem and your dad should be here any minute. The Hamdans are coming, too."

"Yes! Layla hasn't been here in forever!" Sam gave her mother another peck on the cheek. "Did I tell you how beautiful you look today, Mama?"

Her mom lowered her head and gave her an I-know-what-you're-doing look.

"Too much?" Sam asked, leaning in to nudge her mom.

"Yalla. Move your butt." Trying to hide a smile, her mom waved her away. "Go tidy the living room."

"Okay, okay, I'm going," said Sam, laughing.

Theirs definitely wasn't a typical American living room. Shiny alabaster mosaic furniture and picture frames reminded her that although Damascus was thousands of miles away, it was never far. Her parents had imported each piece in shipping containers that took months to arrive. In the corner stood a dresser made of iridescent mother-of-pearl pieces, each perfectly cut and placed alongside polished camel bone to swirl into petal and leaf formations. A pair of ornate armchairs fit for royalty faced a fireplace, above which hung a pearly, mosaic mirror.

Sam shoved the shiny, cut-shell backgammon board under the couch, then arranged the engraved brass arabesque tea set on the top of the buffet.

Sam loved the small boxes that were spread across their coffee table and mantle. Whenever her grandmother visited from Syria, she would bring the most intricate boxes from her mosaic shop. Sam had one that looked like a miniature treasure chest. When they were kids, she and Kareem pretended to be pirates who found secret maps that led to the chest.

The doorbell jolted Sam from her dreamy tidying.

"The Hamdans are here," she called before opening the door. She gave Layla a tight hug and kissed Layla's parents once on each cheek. "Hi, Tant Amira. Hi, Amo Mazen. Mama's in the kitchen, and Baba should be here with Kareem any minute."

Right then, Sam's dad's Volvo pulled into the driveway.

"Ahh, talking of the devil," said Layla's dad.

"Baba." Layla laughed. "It's speak of the devil."

"Iskoutey," said her dad, waving his daughter away. "Quiet. Leave me alone! I don't need English lessons from my fourteen-year-old."

Layla typed something into her phone and showed Sam the screen. "I'm keeping track of all the FOB sayings Mom and Dad come out with. Yesterday, my mom asked me if I wanted to go to King Burger!"

Sam read the list and laughed. "Ha, 'get out of the city' instead of 'get out of town.' 'Joe Trader's,' instead of 'Trader Joe's.' These are awesome! Oh, remember when my mom saw a weeping willow and called it a crying willy? I almost peed myself."

They were still giggling as Kareem got out of the car and straightened his tall frame. Sam gasped, mid-laugh. She'd known he wouldn't be the same skinny eight-year-old she used to play with, but she hadn't expected him to look like a high school sophomore, either. The warm brown eyes she remembered were hidden behind shaggy, dark brown bangs. He wore skinny black jeans and a royal blue hooded soccer sweatshirt. He looked cooler than Sam remembered, sort of European; definitely no longer the geeky Arab kid whose mother dressed him in button-down shirts and loafers.

Kareem lifted his suitcase out of the trunk, awkwardly hoisting his backpack at the same time.

"Sam, your cousin is cute!" whispered Layla.

"He's really changed," whispered Sam, staring at Kareem.

"Samira, come help your cousin," her dad said.

"Oh yeah, of course!" Sam ran down the steps to her cousin and gave Kareem two kisses, Syrian style. "Kareem, keefak?"

It was like kissing a statue.

You're supposed to kiss back. Okayyy.

"Kareem, shtatilak." Sam stepped back and smiled big. "I'm so happy you're here."

"Thanks," Kareem mumbled, before dragging his suitcase to the porch.

Nice to see you, too.

"He's tired, habibti. It has been a long trip." Her dad handed her a small bag from the back seat. "Can you take the rest of his things, please?"

Once they were all inside, Sam's dad proudly introduced Kareem to the Hamdans. Layla's parents leaned over to give Kareem the two kisses, but again, he just stood there. Sam's father's eyebrows were slowly furrowing into what resembled a single, straight, furry caterpillar. This wasn't how people greeted guests, and it certainly wasn't how kids were supposed to greet adults.

"Yalla, habibi, Ahlan, ahlan ya habibi." Sam's dad pointed out the way to the bathroom. The fact Kareem had only just arrived was saving his butt right now. "Welcome. Why don't you clean up and get ready for dinner?"

Sam's mom came out from the kitchen and extended her arms to embrace Kareem. "Nawarit Allansdale, ya Kareem." She planted big kisses on Kareem's cheeks, then pulled back.

Sam smiled. *Allansdale is all lit up!* Arabs really knew how to lay out the welcome mat. There were so many ways to welcome someone and respond appropriately. A single welcome was even made into a hundred welcomes—meyt marhaba. The person being welcomed would return the greeting with even sweeter phrases or place their hand over their heart, as if to physically accept the blessings.

Even though Sam didn't know all the proper ways to respond to the various salutations, she was pretty sure standing there blankly wasn't one of them.

"Marhaba, Tant," Kareem said softly.

"Marbaha, habibi, ahlan wa sahlan," Sam's mom said. "What are they feeding you in Syria? You've gotten so big!" She led him to the living room. "You must be tired. I made you some good food. Yalla, wash up. Dinner is ready, everybody."

Sam and Layla admired the spread. There were dips and pickles. Hummos, muhamarra, pickled turnips, cucumbers, and radishes. Three types of fatayer—meat, cheese, and spinach.

Tabbouleh. Stuffed grape leaves topped with large shanks of meat. And of course, the shishbarak.

"Wow, what a feast." Layla sat next to Sam and grabbed a pillowy cheese-filled pastry. "Tant Ranya, this is amazing!"

Without a word, Kareem took a seat on Sam's other side. When Sam's mom finished serving Layla's parents, she reached for his plate. "Kareem, what can I serve you?"

"I'm not hungry, Tant," he said in Arabic.

"You have to eat, habibi. I'll just put you a little." She scooped some stuffed grape leaves into the middle of the plate, then added a spoonful of hummos and a side of tabbouleh. A few pieces of fatayer went on the other side. She placed the plate back in front of him. "Should I put you a bowl of shishbarak, too?"

Kareem shook his head, picked up his fork, and slowly pushed the food around his plate.

"Kareem, we hear you're a star soccer player," said Amo Mazen.

"He's great," said Sam's dad. "The next Ronaldo."

Kareem didn't look up, his bangs still flopped over his eyes.

Sam leaned over to Layla and whispered, "What's wrong with him?"

Layla shrugged.

"Aww, Kareem, you must be so tired," said Tant Amira. "Our last trip from Gaza to New York took a full forty-eight hours. It's exhausting."

The adults erupted into a discussion of flights and checkpoints and layovers and airports, while Kareem sat there bleary-eyed, not saying anything.

Layla smiled big at him, leaning around Sam. "AMS has a legit soccer team. They just won the state quarterfinals. Sam did the banner for the game. She's a super-talented artist. You should see what she does with letters."

Kareem put down his fork.

"The semifinal's next week," Sam said, trying to sound chipper. "If they win, they'll go to the state finals and then the regionals." She waited for Kareem to acknowledge them. Still nothing. "Maybe you can try out for the team next year. I'm friends with some of the players, and they practice during the summer, too."

"I am not interested," said Kareem without making eye contact.

Anxiety washed over Sam. What was she going to do with this guy? Even if he was tired, this wasn't how you acted when you saw your cousin for the first time in five years.

"He's being a jerk," she whispered to Layla.

"I can hear you, Samira." Kareem's voice was tense.

Sam's eyes narrowed slightly. "Okayyy, then maybe try a little harder."

Kareem stood abruptly and faced the adults. "Khalo Ahmed, Tant Ranya, I am not feeling very well. May I be excused?"

"Of course, habibi." Mrs. Sukkari glanced at her husband. "Ahmed will take you to your room. There are towels on the bed. Let me know if you need anything at all."

"Thank you, Tant. I'm sorry. I'm just . . . really tired."

Kareem followed Sam's dad out. Sam picked out a dumpling from her shishbarak. Normally, each bite was heaven, but suddenly she could barely taste it. Layla was also picking at her food. In fifteen minutes, Kareem had sucked all the scrumptiousness out of dinner.

"Well, that was fun," Sam mumbled.

"Tell me about it." Layla popped a wrapped grape leaf into her mouth, took out her phone, and opened the list of Arab-ish phrases. "Come on, I bet we can think of more." She always knew how to cheer Sam up.

Sam tried to enjoy herself with Layla, but she couldn't stop thinking about Kareem. This wasn't how she remembered him. Like, at all. Her cousin was fun and playful and *funny*. She had no idea who this Kareem was. She knew he'd had to leave his parents and that a revolution was brewing in Syria. People seemed generally excited; some were worried. But her parents had put out the full, adult-sized Arab red carpet, and Kareem had trampled all over it. Her mom produced an entire spread, including the hard stuff—warak 'anab and shishbarak!—but Kareem had been so ungrateful. And rude.

She tried to imagine his name in Arabic, but the letters weren't connected the way they should be. They were rough, disconnected shapes. Sam couldn't make out his letters yet. But she *was* sure she didn't like this Kareem one bit.

CHAPTER 11

KAREEM

Kareem barricaded himself in his new room over the weekend to avoid talking to anyone. His uncle gave him a new cell phone and told him he'd start school on Wednesday because the district was still processing some paperwork. On Monday, he stayed in bed until he was sure everybody had left for the day, then he grabbed his sketchbook and wandered upstairs. He was famished after barely eating all weekend.

He admired the perfectly arranged rows of Tupperware in the fridge. His parents' fridge didn't look like this, but he could recognize similarities—the jars of pickled turnips and labneh, the Tupperware full of hummos. There was leftover shishbarak and basella from another night, but he couldn't be bothered to heat them up. Instead, he grabbed an apple, a few slices of cheese, and some cold cuts, and took them out to the front porch.

He took a deep breath of fresh air and looked at the trees that lined the street's driveways. How many people even lived in this town? It was small, pristine, new. And quiet. He'd never heard a place so quiet in his life. Even the smallest street in Damascus had kids playing and cars honking. Here, there was nothing but crickets and chirping birds.

There were five houses on the entire cul-de-sac. In Damascus, there would be at least ten apartment buildings on a street this size, with twenty stores below, along with a dukkaneh—a kiosk that sold all the snacks and drinks a kid could ask for. And almost everyone knew each other, or at least recognized one another. It was the oldest continually inhabited city in the world. He loved the way its streets were alive with people, with coffee shops and restaurants and taxis and microbuses, at all times of the day. His backyard was a living, breathing museum, with Roman ruins and Islamic architecture alongside bustling souks and businesses, ancient and new, side by side. It was a city always in a loud, kinetic frenzy.

Allansdale couldn't feel more different.

Kareem sat on the front porch swing and opened his sketchbook to the drawing of chains and #WeAreAllHamza. What were Hassan, Yusuf, and George up to now? Were they hanging out without him? He checked his phone. It was about eight o'clock p.m. in Damascus. They'd probably be having dinner.

"Kareem!" A barefoot girl in an owl T-shirt tiptoed up the Sukkaris' gravelly walkway. She had short brown hair with a strip of bright blue bangs, freckles, and a warm smile. "I saw you come outside. I was on my front porch and thought I should say hi." She paused. "Hi."

Kareem's throat was dry from not having spoken in a while. "Hello."

"Do you remember me? We met a million years ago. Well, maybe like five years. But Sam's told me so many stories about you from when you were little. I'm Ellie Gold, Sam's, uhh . . ." She paused and bit her lip. "Sam's best friend. I live across the street. Did I mention we met before?"

Kareem stared at her. She spoke so quickly, Kareem had to really focus to understand what she was saying. Maybe she was nervous? She didn't *look* nervous.

"Sam?" he said, confused. "Who is Sam?"

"Samira," said Ellie.

"But isn't Sam a boy's name?" Kareem frowned. He vaguely remembered her. "And you're Ellie? I have never heard of this name before."

"Well, they're our nicknames. My full name is Eleanora, and you know Sam's is Samira. Sam can be a boy's name. But not necessarily. But that's what everybody calls us— Sam and Ellie. It's been like that since—well, like, forever." She grinned.

As exhausted and angry as he was, Kareem found himself slightly amused. This girl was so direct . . . and odd. There was something refreshing about her.

"Did you lose your shoes?" he asked, smiling despite himself.

"Oh no. I was painting posters for the food pantry where I volunteer, and I rushed over without thinking when I saw you." She blushed. "I'm not big on shoes, though."

"Why aren't you at school?" asked Kareem.

"I've been sick, so I stayed home. Maybe I shouldn't have come over, but I'm not *that* sick. It's a little sniffle. And a cough. And a runny nose. Okay, maybe I'm sick. But I'm totally feeling much better today." Ellie peered at Kareem's sketch. "Wow, that's really good. Did you do that?"

Kareem slammed his sketchbook shut.

"Sorry." Ellie backed up a few steps. "I guess art runs in the family. Sam's amazing at it, and Dr. Sukkari's calligraphy is beautiful." She gestured to his book. "And that was just cool."

"Thanks."

Kareem suddenly wanted to be alone again, but Ellie plunked herself down on the top step and looked at him earnestly. "Can I ask something?"

"You like to ask a lot of questions in America," he said. It came out a little more abrupt than he'd intended.

"Actually, *you've* asked all the questions so far." She paused, as if counting the topics. "You've asked me about my name, my shoes, why I'm not at school. See?"

Kareem found himself smiling again. This girl was definitely different. There were plenty of friendly girls in Damascus, but they wouldn't run across the street barefoot or have blue hair, and they wouldn't be this . . . forward?

"Who's Hamza?" she asked, interrupting his thoughts.

Kareem's throat tightened, and he stood. "I have to go, Eleanora."

"Oh, I'm sorry." She scrambled to her feet as well, twisting her fingers together. "I didn't mean to . . . I'm sorry." She pointed toward her house. "Hey, remember my treehouse? My dad built it. You loved it when you visited. Want to check it out again?"

Through the trees, Kareem could see a tan, circus-style canopy. He *did* remember it. His last visit came back to him in a rush—he'd been so excited to come to the United States and go to Disneyland. When he'd first seen that treehouse, he'd almost lost his mind. He couldn't believe a father would build a real-life treehouse for his daughter. He'd thought such things only existed in cartoons and movies. How could he have forgotten about it?

"So, wanna come over?" Ellie asked, her expression hopeful.

"I have to go," Kareem said. "See you later, Eleanora."

"Okay, well, it's there anytime you want to visit. Mi treehouse es su treehouse." Ellie grinned and waved as she headed back across the street. "See ya!"

Kareem waved back. Remembering the treehouse had brought his last trip back so vividly—but this time was different. He wasn't here on vacation. He'd been sent away. And, anyway, he wasn't that kid anymore.

CHAPTER 12

SAMIRA

Cat Spencer's voice blared through the hallways' speakers, announcing the new Spirit Squad banner competition, as Sam made her way to her third-period class on Wednesday.

"The team that creates the banner to best represent our school's spirit will be featured in the *Allansdale Gazette*. You'll become world-famous! Okay, Allansdale-famous. But that's not all! The winners get the chance to run the school for a day. You heard me! Whatever you say, goes."

Avery and Lucy jumped on Sam from behind, and Lucy gave her a big hug. "Are you ready to rule the school?"

"We're submitting a banner? When did this happen?" Sam twisted a curl furiously. "I mean, we're in Spirit Squad, are we even allowed?"

"It's totally fine, because the teachers are voting, not Spirit Squad!" said Lucy.

"We need to start meeting after school again," Avery said. "Didn't Cat tell you?"

Sam swallowed hard. "Umm, no, she didn't."

"Oh yeah, I totally forgot to tell you," said Cat, dropping her backpack in the middle of their semicircle. She smiled at the other two girls. "I killed that announcement, didn't I?"

"How did you get here so fast?" said Avery, giggling. "It's like you're everywhere!" She paused. "Oh, and you totally killed it."

Cat curtsied.

"Sam, you're totally our secret weapon!" said Lucy. "We're going to win this thing!"

"I wouldn't be so sure," Dylan said, coming up behind them. "The soccer team is making one, too, and we've got our *own* secret weapon." He pointed to Amari, who was busting photo poses, left, then right, then left again.

"And, of course," added Dylan, bowing, "we've got me!"

Sam smiled. She couldn't help it. He was just so . . . confident . . . and . . .

"Sam, you're blushing," whispered Lucy in Sam's ear.

Sam tried to shake away the redness, looking back and forth from Dylan to Amari. "Are you sure you've got the right guy? Your secret weapon, I mean."

"You have no idea," said Dylan. "He's like the next . . . the next . . . you know, whoever's the most famous artist guy. Picasso, or whatever."

"I'm more like the next Banksy." Amari paused to think. "No, the next Seen UA."

"Who's Seen UA?" asked Cat, gazing bright-eyed at Amari.

"Only the most famous graffiti artist in the world," said Sam. "Mr. Modest here thinks he's the godfather of graffiti."

Amari looked at her, surprised. Well, he'd surprised her, too. She hadn't expected someone so silly and loud to know about a graffiti artist from the 1970s. She'd learned about Seen UA—and how he started graffitiing NYC subways cars at only eleven—when she was researching why she pictured people as letters. She and Amari smiled at each other, and Sam felt her ears turn red.

"I love his letters," she said. "I'm sort of obsessed with everything letters."

"Me too!" said Amari, his smile growing. "His stuff is fire!"

Cat crossed her arms and raised an eyebrow. "You love his letters?" She stared them both down. "Okay, this convo is getting weird. I'm outta here." She turned to leave, adding, "By the way, Sam, we're meeting after school on Monday."

A lump formed in Sam's throat. Not only was she still grounded, her parents had no idea she was part of Spirit Squad. She stared at her shoes, wishing she could disappear. "I, uh, don't t-think I can," she stammered. "I'm sort of grounded."

"So we'll come to your house. Okay? Perfect." Cat swung her bag onto her shoulder and smiled at Amari. "Bye, Amari, see you in math."

A wave of panic came over Sam. How would she explain Spirit Squad to her parents? She could hear her father's voice in her head: *What is this? My daughter wants to be a cheerleader?*

Over my dead body. It only got worse when Avery whispered, "By the way, I met your cousin this morning. He's cuuutte!"

Sam had almost managed to forget about Kareem. She'd barely slept the previous night worrying about how her cranky, unpleasant cousin would fit into her AMS world.

She took in a deep breath and closed her eyes as the bell rang.

"Hey, why so serious all of a sudden?" asked Amari.

Sam opened her eyes. The others were all hurrying to class, except Amari, who was just standing there looking at her.

"I'm not," said Sam, flustered. She smiled. "I'm fine. Just late. Get a move on, Banksy!"

All of them were going to meet Kareem soon, and Cat had just invited the whole Spirit Squad to her house. Her world suddenly felt too small.

CHAPTER 13

KAREEM

Kareem sat in the bright classroom, drawing on the scratch paper he had been given for his math assessment. The teacher had told him the assessment would take at least an hour, but he'd finished in twenty minutes. Total breeze. If this was the standard, he would definitely make the honors program, and his parents and uncle would be ecstatic. Even that simple thought made his stomach churn. How long was he going to be in Allansdale?

He sketched out his newest piece: a boy trying to push over a giant wall with his bare hands. In Arabic, above, he wrote "Qawim." *Resist.* He wondered what his friends would say about this one. He was pretty sure even Hassan would be okay with it.

The teacher sat at her desk, marking papers. This school was nothing like Kareem's back home. At the front of the room hung some sort of fancy television instead of a simple chalkboard. The hallways were bright, with a mural of the sky painted above a sea of turquoise lockers. The desks in the class-rooms were bare. Kareem had expected students to leave one another messages, drawings, and scribbles, but there was nothing. Did someone clean them every night? Or were American kids not bored at school?

"Kareem, are you done already? How was it?"

"It was fine, Miss.

"Mrs. Caldwell," the teacher finished with a smile.

"Mrs. Caldwell." A bit embarrassed, Kareem handed her the paper. In Syria, teachers were simply called Miss or Mrs. Or maybe Ms. Amy or Mrs. Maha. Last names weren't used.

She flipped through the test. "Well, you can join the seventh and eighth graders for lunch now."

Kareem stuffed the drawing into his backpack to replicate later in his sketchbook and headed for the cafeteria. The hallways felt huge and empty and lonely. Then he opened the cafeteria doors, and an avalanche of noise hit him.

He marveled at the size of the room. The cafeteria at his Syrian school was small and dim, with only a few round tables. Most kids didn't eat there. This one had dozens of large, rectangular tables, with hundreds of kids all talking and laughing at once. At the far end, a banner read ALLANSDALE MIDDLE SCHOOL—2010–2011—LIONS ROAR.

Kareem had ten dollars his uncle had stuffed into his jacket pocket that morning. He joined the lunch line and looked at the steaming food being served. He had no idea how to order. What would he say? Can I have some yellow goop, please? Is there meat under that brown sauce? What are those tiny green trees?

He shoved his tray down the line and grabbed a piece of fruit and a cookie, then made his way through the sea of tables, searching for a quiet place to sit.

A hand lightly tapped his arm, and he jumped.

"Kareem, hey," said Sam. "I didn't mean to startle you." She was at a table with three boys and three other girls. Ellie wasn't among them.

Maybe she's still sick.

"How's it going?" Sam asked brightly. She looked nervous.

"I'm okay," said Kareem, his voice monotone.

One of the girls tilted her head toward him with a big smile. "Hi, I'm Cat. Sam, aren't you going to introduce us?"

"Everyone, this is my cousin Kareem," said Samira. "He's new to AMS."

A barrage of hellos and introductions hit Kareem. Cat moved across to make space. "Sit with us."

Reluctantly, Kareem sat.

"So, where did you come from?" asked Cat, watching him intently.

"Syria."

"Oh, I haven't heard of that school," said Cat.

Amari laughed. "It's a country, Cat."

Cat's jaw locked, and she flushed a little. "Yeah, duh. I knew that. I was just joking."

"Aren't there protests or something happening there now?" Amari asked him. "My parents were talking about it the other day."

Kareem nodded. "A revolution. There are protests all over the country."

"Is that why you left?" asked Dylan. "My dad says people over there have been at war for centuries. It's, like, in their blood or something."

Kareem felt his face flush. He clenched his teeth.

In their blood? Who is this jerk?

He waited for Samira to say something, but she was picking at her food, avoiding eye contact with anyone. How could she just let the comment about "people over there" slide? Kareem looked at the girl who had thought Syria was a *school*. She was sitting next to Sam, silent, her eyes narrowed. How could his own cousin be friends with these people?

Kareem lifted his chin to stare at Dylan. "It's not a war, it's a revolution. You should look up the difference. So ignorant."

"He didn't mean it that way, Kareem." Samira glanced back and forth between them, her expression panicky.

"Yeah, I didn't mean it that way," said Dylan. "I mean, it's just what my dad says. A lot of people say that. But it's, whatever, right?"

Kareem looked at Dylan in disbelief.

"Mari'ha," Samira whispered. She raised her eyebrows and made her eyes wide, in Syrian eye-language for *please, let's talk about it later, move on.* "Ma'lishey, moo azdo."

Let it go? Kareem seethed. She was basically defending this idiot. How dare she tell *him* to let it go?

"I have a question for you, Samira Sukkari," said Kareem loudly. "Why does everybody call you Sam when you have a beautiful *Arabic* name? Samira." He rolled the R in her name for emphasis and watched the color drain from her face. "Your name is Samee-rrr-a. If you'd prefer to use a boy's name, then Samer, with a rrrr"—Kareem trilled the sound—"would be the appropriate Arabic version. That's what you need, right? An Arab, Syrian, Muslim name? Or would that make your friends think you love to fight? Because it's in your blood?" He looked at Dylan, nostrils flared.

"Kareem, what are you talking about?" hissed Sam.

"You know exactly what, Samira Sukkari."

"Seriously, what is wrong with you?" Samira leaped up, grabbed her sweater, and bolted out of the cafeteria.

Dylan stood. "What's your problem, man? Sam can use whatever name she wants. It's cool. Talk about a hater."

"You don't understand why she changes her name?" Kareem said, his anger boiling in his chest. "Obviously, because she goes to school with ignorant people like you."

Dylan looked around the table, which had gone completely silent, then back at Kareem. "Wow," he said loudly, so that even the tables around them fell silent. "Maybe you should go back to Syria. This isn't how we treat people in America."

Kareem stood up and walked out. Behind him, he heard only one boy's voice saying, "Dylan! What the heck?"

Kareem scanned the empty corridors for Samira, but she was nowhere to be found. Maybe he had taken it too far, wanting to embarrass her and shame them all. And he knew he'd been rude since arriving in Allansdale. But he didn't want to be here. His blood boiled. He tried to think what George and Hassan would say. Hassan would have told him to walk away, not to engage. But sometimes, Kareem couldn't help himself. The words came out like someone else was saying them.

Kareem ducked into a bathroom and shut himself in a stall. How was he going to live in this town, go to this school, be around these people? When would his parents let him go *home*?

CHAPTER 14

SAMIRA

Sam ran straight to the last stall in the girls' bathroom. She slammed the door shut over and over again, fighting back tears.

She hadn't really wanted to call Kareem over in the cafeteria, but he looked so sad and lost and pathetic, wandering between the tables. She wanted to help. And she'd barely seen him since he arrived. She'd convinced herself that maybe his crankiness was just jet lag.

Now she was sure—he wasn't tired, jet-lagged, or homesick. He was a jerk. Okay, Dylan shouldn't have said what he did, but you can't just lose it every time someone says something ignorant. And why did Kareem care if people called her Sam? She pulled out her cell phone.

Sam

Are you there??

Sam

LAYLA . . . Please answer me!

Sam

WHERE ARE YOU??

Sam

NEED YOU ASAP!!

Layla

On my way to lunch. You okay?

Sam

Kareem picked a fight with Dylan and totally embarrassed me in front of the entire seventh and eighth grade. :(

Layla

What did he do?

Sam typed out everything that had happened, thumbs flying.

Layla

WHAT? Sounds like they were all being jerks, actually.

Sam

I'm in a bathroom stall, bawling.

Layla

Aww, Samira. Don't cry. He's not worth it.

Sam

You would have known what to say. ☹
I wish you were here.

Layla

Don't feel bad, Sam. He's the one who looked like a jerk. Gotta go—don't let him get to you!

Sam put her phone away and left the stall to wash her face just as Avery and Lucy came in.

"We've been looking for you everywhere," said Lucy. "Are you okay?"

"Yeah, I'm fine."

"You know, I love the name Samira. It's beautiful. You should totally use it." Lucy looked at Avery, who was silent. "I mean, if you want to, of course. But Samira is really pretty." She paused uncomfortably. "I guess I just wanted to tell you that."

"Thanks, Lucy." Sam dried her face, trying to hold back tears.

In truth, Sam knew she had a beautiful name. She had only changed it after being mocked with "Samira-the-weirda" all through third grade. On top of teasing her about her "weird" lunches, she'd had enough. She'd been Sam ever since.

When Sam told her parents she didn't want to be called Samira anymore, they'd listened patiently. Then they told her the story of her name. Her dad explained that every Arabic word had a three-letter root—Samira's were Sa, Ma, and Ra. The word meant "to sit and talk to someone into the night."

They had tried for years to have a baby before she arrived. She was an only child because they struggled to conceive, her dad told her.

Her mom took over. "After seven years, I had basically given up. Then one night, I dreamed that a little girl with dark brown curls—I couldn't see her face, but I saw her curls—sat with me beside a lake. She talked late into the night about her favorite toys and foods and movies. She told me she wanted to build things and create magical works of art when she grew up. And then she asked if I could take her to the playground, and I woke up."

Sam's parents held hands all through the story.

"The next morning, your mom told me she had met our little girl." Her dad had a huge smile on his face. "I thought she'd dreamed it because she was so desperate, but two weeks later, we learned she was pregnant. Your mom already knew. And she had already given you a name: Samira, the beloved friend with whom you have late-night conversations."

"So, habibti," her mom said, "we knew you were Samira even before you were born. In this house, that is your name."

Sam loved the story. She wondered if she had actually chosen her own name. That night, she decided she would be Samira at home.

Third grade was a long time ago, and sometimes she considered going back to Samira, but it felt like a hassle. Plus, she had grown to love the name Sam. She liked controlling who she was. She liked having school-Sam and home-Samira. It was clear and defined and perfect.

But now Kareem had broken down that tidy barrier of hers, making an ugly mess of it and showing it to everyone—including Cat Spencer, and Dylan. She wished Dylan hadn't said those things, but still, they could have talked to him about it, maybe. Now it was gnawing at her, though—she'd been so uncomfortable, and then so angry with Kareem, that she hadn't even processed how much Dylan's comments bothered her.

"My cousin didn't used to be like this," Sam told Lucy and Avery. She was furious with Kareem, but she still felt compelled to defend him. Her parents had hammered home that they didn't discuss family with the outside world. "I don't know what's up with him."

"He seems like a mega jerk," said Avery sympathetically.

Even though Sam wasn't supposed to agree, she nodded.

"You won't believe what happened after you left," said Lucy.

Sam's horror grew as Lucy and Avery took turns filling her in. It was nice that Dylan stood up for her, even though he obviously didn't understand what was happening in Syria. But telling Kareem to go back to where he came from was *not* okay.

"Oh my God," said Sam, twirling her hair nervously. "Why does this kind of thing always happen to me?"

Lucy gave Sam a big hug. As Sam hugged back, she found herself wishing that Lucy was Ellie at that moment. Lucy was super nice, but Ellie understood. She'd been through it all with her. She really wanted one of those long, late-night talks they had during sleepovers. She needed her best friend.

Sam entered quietly through the back door and hung her jacket in the mudroom. She'd managed to avoid Kareem for the rest of the day.

"Hi, habibti," her mom called. "How was school?"

"Hi, Mama. Hi, Baba." Sam found them in the kitchen chopping vegetables for dinner and gave them kisses. "It was fine." She grabbed an apple, desperately hoping to get away before the inevitable next question.

"How was Kareem's first day?" asked her dad. "Did you see him?"

What could she say? *He was terrible. He embarrassed me in front of all my friends. I think my cousin is a jerk.*

"I saw him once," she eventually said. "He seemed fine."

Her father lifted an eyebrow, his head tilted, and one hand turned upward with fingers fanned out. The universal Arabic sign for "And? So?" Sam pictured Layla in the same posture and snickered.

"Why don't you just ask *him* how it was?" she said.

"He came home and went straight downstairs," her mom said. "He's very tired. The jet lag."

"Yeah, right," Sam said under her breath. "Jet lag."

"What was that, habibti?"

"Nothing, Mama." Sam shouldered her backpack. "I have homework."

She paused, suddenly remembering Spirit Squad was coming to her house on Monday. How to ask for permission? Should she tell her parents it was for an art project? Or maybe it was time to come clean. But after what happened last week, there was no way they'd be okay with her joining the team.

Her father looked up from his onions. "Habibti, do you need something?"

Sam hated lying to them. But this was so small, it really wasn't a big deal.

"Um, we got assigned a big group project for science. Since I'm grounded, is it okay if my group comes over on Monday afternoon to work on it?" When her parents hesitated, she added, "It'll only take an hour. Two, max."

Sam's mom looked at her dad, then said, "Fine, but only because it is for school."

"You're still grounded," said her dad.

"Understood." Sam hugged them both and ran upstairs, planning how to prepare for guests. Maybe she could make brownies. Definitely no adameh ala sukkar this time.

A knock at the door. Sam's parents never knocked. As far as they were concerned, her door didn't exist.

"Samira, are you in there?"

Kareem. She cringed. Hadn't he done enough today? She didn't want to deal with him.

"What do you want?" Sam snapped.

"Please open. I need to talk with you."

Sam opened the door. Kareem was tapping his foot on the soft carpet, his arms behind his back. He looked more disheveled than he had at lunch, like he'd just woken up from a nap. He stood there silently, looking at her.

"Yes?" asked Sam. She raised her eyebrows and crossed her arms. "Can I help you?"

"Samira, why didn't you say something to those kids at school?" Kareem asked. For the first time since his arrival in the US, he looked Sam straight in the eyes. "Why would you let them say those things about us?"

Sam sighed. How could she explain this to her cousin, who had been in the United States for just a few days? He had no idea what it was like to grow up in America. No one had ever made fun of his name or called him a terrorist. He'd never seen people look at his hijab-wearing mom with suspicion or disgust.

"Kareem, you just don't get it," Sam said, exasperated. "You don't know what it's like being the only Muslim and Arab kid in school. In the *town*. You can't pick a fight with every person who says something ignorant."

"So you sit there and let them say whatever nonsense they want?" asked Kareem, his nostrils flared.

"What am I supposed to do, Kareem? Give them a history lesson? Or maybe a geography lesson? Wait, that was a politics lesson. Why don't we get a chalkboard and set up in the cafeteria? And then—"

"You can't say nothing when people insult you that way, Samira Sukkari," interrupted Kareem. "This is just not acceptable."

"Well, *you* sure handled it well," said Sam. She wanted to slam the door in her cousin's face. "Now the entire school thinks Arabs are jerks!"

Sam's eyes welled up again. She knew she should have said something to Dylan. She had wanted to. But her mouth always dried up in those moments, and her words always failed her. They stood there facing each other for a few more seconds in awkward silence. Then Kareem shook his head in disgust, turned around, and marched downstairs.

Once Kareem was gone, Sam allowed the hot tears to pour down her face. She picked up her phone, thought for a minute, then flopped onto her bed, burying herself in her covers. She wished she could call Ellie again. How could she be fighting with her cousin and best friend at the same time?

"Why are they both so . . . ," she yelled into her pillow, "JUDGY!"

CHAPTER 15

KAREEM

Kareem rocked on the porch swing, enjoying the sun's rays. It was Sunday, and the house was empty. Khalo Ahmed had asked him to join Samira at Sunday school, but he didn't feel like making small talk. Tant Ranya was out grocery shopping. Kareem was grateful to have the house to himself, even if for only a few hours.

He leaned back and thought about his disastrous first few days of school. Not only was everybody still gossiping about his outburst, now he was fighting with his cousin. He hadn't meant to start a full-blown argument. He just wanted her to stand up for herself, for who she was. He thought he wouldn't care that she was upset with him. But he did.

Kareem opened Twitter and scrolled through his feed, which was exploding with messages, pictures, and videos. #Syria, #Syrianrevolution, #free_Syria. Protesters had taken to the streets of Homs. One headline read: STUDENTS IN INSHA'AT AND BAB AMRO IN HOMS, and below it was a photo of hundreds of people holding a single Syrian flag that spanned blocks. Kareem beamed as he watched a clip of the scene. That flag was huge! The people were chanting the same line he had chanted just a few weeks ago: "Al Sha'ab Youreed Isqaat al Nizam, Al Sha'ab Youreed Isqaat al Nizam, Al Sha'ab Youreed Isqaat al Nizam."

Kareem's heart fluttered, almost as if he was there again.

Another tweet said students in Dara'a were protesting with: "No studies, no lessons, until the regime falls!" Those in Masaken Barzeh were chanting, "He who fights the people is a traitor!"

Kareem carefully studied the footage. It was close to his mama and baba's hospital.

Tweet after tweet showed a new place, a new protest, a new set of flags and signs and posters and chants. It was like the entire country was out. He stopped at a post of graffiti on a large wall. The word "Freedom" was written in the colors of the Syrian flag and underneath, #SprayMan.

Spray Man? Who's Spray Man? The image had been shared hundreds of times. He searched the hashtag and found a dozen other pieces. Mostly words. "Freedom for Syria." "Freedom Now." "Free Syria."

Kareem stood up and kept scrolling through the tweets as if in a trance. Were his friends there? He checked their accounts. They had all made secret accounts with fake names when they'd started graffitiing. Hassan's was ShamGram—he'd chosen it since Sham was what Syrians called Damascus. Were they working on new pieces without him? Kareem scratched his neck—his skin tingled with excitement, even though he was nowhere near it. He didn't know what to do with himself, so he texted Hassan.

Kareem

What's up? Did you go to the party today?

He used studying to mean graffiti, but they had never really created a code for protests. "Party" seemed like a good one. He hoped Hassan would understand what he meant.

Hassan

It was awesome.

Kareem smiled. *Even Hassan went! How cool.*

Kareem

How about studying? Did you have a test today?

Hassan

Yes! But it's getting harder.

Kareem nodded.

Kareem

I miss you, Hassan.

Hassan

I miss you too.

Kareem searched through his pictures and found a drawing that depicted a boy pushing down a wall. He wished he could send it to Hassan. He couldn't. That would only put Hassan in potential danger.

Hassan

Gotta go, mama's calling me.

Kareem

Okay. Keep studying!

Hassan

Bye!!

Kareem thought about his own parents. He'd only spoken with them once, when he first arrived. They'd called twice since then, but Kareem was still so angry that he'd pretended to be asleep both times. Suddenly he missed them. A lot. He needed to make sure they were okay.

Kareem

Mama, how are you? How is Baba? Are you okay?

He waited patiently for a reply. Nothing.

They're probably just busy in the hospital.

The protests, the graffiti, his parents, his cousin. Kareem paced back and forth on the porch. He didn't know whether to jump up and down for joy for Hassan or scream in anger at Allansdale. Syrians were coming out in droves, just like Ramy had said they would, but he was stuck in Massachusetts, fighting with his cousin about some kids who didn't even know where Syria was on a map. He was in the wrong place, at the wrong time, with the wrong people. Everything felt off.

"Hey, Kareem!" Ellie glided up the Sukkari driveway on her bike. "Look, I have shoes on today!" She hopped off her bike and kicked her feet into the air to show him her glittery silver Converse.

"I'm so happy you found them," said Kareem, solemnly.

Ellie smiled and trotted up to the porch. "I'd ask how school's going, but I already heard. You really made a splash in your first week, didn't you? Impressive."

Kareem lowered his head. So people were talking.

"Whoa, Kareem, that is really amazing." Ellie walked around to take a better look at his sketchbook. This time, Kareem didn't bother to close it. He'd spent ages last night redrawing the lonely boy as three boys, pushing with all their might against a high brick wall. Another boy sat to the side, his shoulders slumped, watching from afar.

"It's so . . ." Ellie paused as she thought of the right word. "Powerful. The look on this boy's face. What does it say?"

"Qawim."

"In English?"

"What's the word—it's when you push something back?" He thought a little more. "Resist! Yes, that is it. Resist."

"What are they resisting? The government?"

Kareem nodded.

Ellie pointed to the boy on the side. "Is that one you?"

"Yes." Tears leaked from his eyes. He turned and wiped them away. "And those are my friends."

"I'm sorry, Kareem." Ellie's eyes filled with tears as well. "After I saw your last picture, I googled Hamza. It's so sad. I can't believe what happened to those boys. And then I read about the protests, and it's all so . . . terrible. But exciting at the same time?"

"People here don't even know Syria is a country," Kareem said, thinking of Cat and Dylan. "They don't know what's happening."

Ellie looked at Kareem's sketch, then she started to pace. "Kareem, maybe . . . maybe we should show them. We could enter a banner in the banner contest."

Kareem frowned. He didn't know anything about making banners, but he did know—

"Grafitti!"

"Okayyy," said Ellie.

His fingers tingled at the idea.

"That's what I did in Syria. I would sketch these pictures, and me and my friends would figure out how to put them on a building or a wall. Usually we just did words, but the last two had pictures."

Ellie's face went white, and her eyes widened. "We can't go around painting buildings in Allansdale. We'll get in big trouble."

"That's the point! We have something to say, so we have to say it in ink. Big. Where everybody can see it."

Ellie shook her head. "We just can't do that here, Kareem. Sorry."

Kareem pressed his lips together. For a moment, he'd felt alive again, like maybe he could do something important. But of course they couldn't, not in pristine Allansdale. He examined the wall he had drawn. What would the "wall" be here, anyway? No one would get it.

"Wait, I have an idea!" Ellie's face lit up. "We can use spray chalk! I use it when we do drives for the homeless shelter."

"Chalk? Like what the teachers use at school?" Kareem asked incredulously.

"Yeah, but spray chalk looks exactly like paint." She was practically bouncing with excitement. "It's bright and it totally works, but it disappears when it rains, so at least we wouldn't go to juvie for it."

"Juvie?"

"Juvenile detention. Jail for kids. I mean, they probably wouldn't send us to jail, but you know what I mean."

Kareem smiled at her excitement. "Yes. I don't want to go to juvie."

"So what do you think? It'll be so cool . . . and fun . . . and did I say cool?"

Kareem thought of Hassan, Yusuf, and George. What would they say? Was this just silly? Hassan probably would have preferred spray paint made from chalk to the real thing. Kareem chuckled without meaning to.

"What are you laughing at?"

"I was thinking what my friends would say about this."

"They'd say this is so COOL!" said Ellie, jumping up and down. "Come over! I'll show you what cans I have, and we can get more if we need. We can even buy some real paint to practice with. Then maybe we can work on our first . . . what do you call them?"

"I guess it's our first piece," said Kareem. "Or maybe a burner."

"Really? A burner?"

"That might be wrong. I read that online." Kareem grinned at her. "In Syria, we just call it grra-ffee-tee. It's really new there." He tucked his sketchbook under his arm. "We'll need a tag, too. A name to sign on our pieces."

"You mean our burners." Ellie was beaming. "How about Karellie? You know, Ellie and Kareem, together." She paused. "No, too obvious. How about Eleem, or . . . GraffitiBombers! Or TalkingTruth or ThisIsYourWorld." She bounded back to her bike. "I'm good at this! I knew I had a revolutionary in me. Like Che. No, Susan B. Anthony. Harriet Tubman. But we're not running an Underground Railroad. Ooh, Rosa Luxemburg. Have you heard of her? She was Polish-Jewish, but also German, and she started this thing called the Spartacus League . . ."

Kareem listened to Eleanora talk and talk, smiling. He'd never heard of Rosa Luxemburg, but Eleanora really knew a lot about her. He loved that this girl knew her story.

"Come on," Ellie said, "I'll show you the spray chalk."

Kareem hesitated. "Wait, is it okay for me to come over?"

"Of course." Ellie rode across the street to her house, dropped her bike on the lawn, and opened the front door.

Kareem followed slowly. Going to a girl's house alone would *not* be allowed in Syria. Not when the family didn't know, and not alone.

"Hurry up, Kareem!" Ellie called. "We have a revolution to start. In Allansdale!"

Kareem laughed. This girl really did talk quickly. His phone buzzed.

Mom

> We're fine, habibi. It has been a long day. We'll call tomorrow. Love you.

He exhaled. Everybody was okay. He hurried across the street after Ellie.

"A revolution in Massachusetts. That would be . . . something."

CHAPTER 16

SAMĪRA

Sam took a deep sniff of the cooling brownies on the stove.

"They're ready!" She sliced into the gooey chocolate layer. "I need to try them to make sure they're cooked through."

"Of course you do," said her mom.

Sam smiled. For the first time in days, things felt normal with her parents. She popped a sliver of brownie in her mouth, huffing and puffing as she chewed the piping hot morsel.

She'd rushed straight home from school to prepare for her friends' arrival. Her mom had suggested the living room to work on the banner. Sam agreed, but quietly decided her room would be better, for privacy's sake. She hated telling another white lie, but she swore to herself that it would be the last time.

She plated the brownies, took them into the living room, and placed them on the coffee table. Her stomach tightened. Why couldn't they have normal couches like everybody else? Why did her living room look like it came from a pearl colony at the bottom of the ocean?

Sam yawned. She'd been restless last night, thinking about what type of letters represented AMS. She associated lettering with individual people, not groups. And definitely not a community that included buildings, teachers, and an entire student body. For so long, AMS had been a boxy, rectangular, almost prison-like place for her. But it was changing. She needed to capture its three-dimensional elements. The banner had to be fun and colorful, or how else would they win?

So she'd stayed up late, researching banners and fonts for inspiration. She found herself admiring graffiti murals and reading about the world's most popular graffiti artists. One of them, eL Seed, used Arabic calligraphy for pieces that sometimes spanned dozens of buildings. They were the coolest pieces she had ever seen. One spanned fifty buildings—each one was amazing by itself, but together, it was a masterpiece. Her father would love it!

Her dad was one of the reasons she loved fonts so much. Ever since she could remember, she had watched him in the corner of his office, bent over reams of paper, with a thin reed brush and a black inkwell. His obsession with Arabic calligraphy had been the beginning of her own fascination with the way letters were formed.

The doorbell rang. Sam bolted from the living room, but her mom beat her to the door. She was already greeting Sam's guests with a big Middle Eastern welcome.

"Hello, ladies," said her mom, smiling extra big. "Welcome, welcome. We're so happy you are here. It's so nice to meet you all."

"Hi." Cat walked in without looking up from her cell phone, followed by Lucy and Avery.

Sam's mom's smile faded. Sam had tried countless times to explain that kids in the US were different. But she knew her mom found it totally unacceptable.

"Hi, Mrs. Sukkari," said Lucy, with a meek smile.

With her mom's gaze boring into them, Sam herded her friends through to the living room. "Let's go. We'll have brownies in here, then we can work in my room."

The doorbell rang again as they were digging into their brownies.

"Is anybody else coming?" Sam asked.

"James said he might be able to make it," mumbled Avery around a mouthful of brownie. "Maybe it's him?"

Sam's eyes widened. She hadn't warned her parents that any boys might be coming. Sam rushed back to the door, a brownie in the palm of her hand, but her mom got there first again.

"Samira, it's Noora!" cried her mom. "How are you, habibti? I've missed you!"

Long ago, Sam's mom had made Ellie an honorary family member by giving her an Arabic nickname. Her mom said it was perfect because not only did it sound like Eleanora, but the Arabic name also meant light. And Ellie was all light. Sam had been embarrassed at first, but Ellie absolutely loved it. It was one of the things that made their friendship so easy—how they could fit into each other's families.

"I've missed you too, Mrs. Sukkari." Ellie gave her the Syrian two kisses, one on each cheek, and a big hug. Then she looked at Sam.

"Hi, Sam," she said, her voice barely audible. She looked down at her sparkly Converse.

"Hi." Sam didn't know what to say. *Is she here to apologize?*

"Mrs. Sukkari, I'm . . . I'm actually here for Kareem," Ellie said, breaking the awkward silence. "We're working on a project together. Is he home?"

Sam's eyebrows furrowed.

Kareem?

Mrs. Sukkari raised her own eyebrow in confusion. "Let me call him for you, habibti."

She headed to the kitchen, leaving Sam and Ellie standing in silence. Sam had so many questions. What project? When had they even had a chance to hang out? Was Kareem actually being nice to her?

"Umm, how's it going?" she said instead.

"Fine," said Ellie, avoiding eye contact. "I smell brownies."

"I actually have friends over now." Sam pointed to the living room. "But, umm, want a brownie?"

Ellie looked over Sam's shoulder and, just as Sam's mom reappeared, she said flatly, "Oh, Spirit Squad. Fun."

Right then Sam wanted to scream. Why did she have to mention Spirit Squad?

"What did you say, Noora?" her mom asked, looking suspiciously at Samira.

"Oh, I just . . . ," Ellie faltered, realizing she'd said something wrong.

"She noticed I'm working on our science project with the Spirit Squad," Sam said, smiling innocently at her mom.

Before her mom could ask another question, Kareem ran past and out the door. "Let's go, Eleanora. Yalla!"

Ellie followed him. "Bye, Mrs. Sukkari."

"Bye, habibti. Come back for dinner?"

"Thanks, but I'm going out with my dad tonight." Ellie glanced at Sam. "Have fun with your . . . uhh . . . science project."

When Ellie had gone, Sam's mom crossed her arms. "We'll talk about this later, Samira. I don't know what's going on here, but we're not done."

Sam nodded. Things had just improved with her parents, and now she'd have to undergo another round of questioning about Spirit Squad. She went back to the living room, suddenly wishing the girls weren't there. She missed Ellie so much, but Ellie was obviously still stewing—and still judging. And Kareem looked happy for the first time since he'd arrived.

Since when are they hanging out? He's been here all of ten days.

Cat pressed her lips together. "What did *she* want?"

"She came by for Kareem," said Sam quietly.

"Oooooh, they'd make a great match. They're both so . . . friendly."

Sam smiled uncomfortably.

"So, this living room is . . ." Cat paused to find the right word. "It's really . . . something."

Sam looked around the room, wishing it would all somehow glimmer a little less. "I can't argue with that." She took a bite of her brownie, sat down beside Lucy, and changed the subject. "So anyway, I've been thinking about themes we might use for the banner."

"Oh, I already decided that," said Cat. "I want it to say, 'Lions Are #1! GRRRRR.'"

"Really?" Sam looked at Avery and Lucy to gauge their reactions, but Avery was concentrating on her brownie, and Lucy was studying the mosaic boxes.

"It's about Spirit Squad," Cat continued. "And spirit is about winning. We just need a cool design that shows we're the best!"

Sam imagined big, bold, winning letters, but couldn't help thinking, *Bo-ringgg.*

"Sam, what are these boxes?" Lucy asked. "They're so cool."

Sam picked up a hexagonal box and smiled. "I know, right? This one's my favorite." She flipped it around to show them the layers of triangles and shapes along its rim. "My grandmother sells them in Syria. Some of them are really old. They're like little treasure chests."

"They totally are," Lucy said, nodding. "I love this one. It almost sparkles."

"Okay, ladies, we don't have time to admire little boxes all day." Cat rolled her eyes. "I have to go, and we have to figure this banner out."

Sam finished her brownie and dusted the crumbs off her fingers.

"Let's move to my room."

Upstairs, Cat and Avery sat on Sam's bed, while Lucy sat beside Sam on the floor.

Sam rolled out a piece of paper. "Okay, so . . . 'We're #1,' with a lion picture? That's pretty straightforward, I guess. But haven't we already done it? It's sort of the same as the soccer—"

"Just change the lion a little," Cat interrupted. She checked her phone. "Make it cool, you know? We're Spirit Squad. We'll definitely win with that. You'll make it look great!"

"Right." This theme was so obvious. "Are you guys sure that's what you want to do?"

"It's the best option," Cat said, confidently. "Okay, you guys have this. I gotta go."

Sam trailed behind her to the front door. Cat kept her head buried in her phone the whole way, even when she passed Sam's mom, and let the door slam behind her. Sam cringed. She could have at least said bye to her mom, who was already shaking her head in disapproval. It was the kind of violation her mom would mention when she accused Sam of becoming "too American." When her parents said that, they really meant disrespectful or spoiled.

When Sam got back to her room, Avery and Lucy were busy playing with the boxes on her dresser.

"Do you guys really like the 'We're #1' idea?" Sam asked.

They both shrugged.

"I'm not crazy about it," Lucy said, "but I guess Cat's right. It is a Spirit Squad thing."

"Yeah," said Avery. "Whatever. If it's what she wants, I think we should just do it. She usually knows what's best."

"Okay, then." Sam flopped on the carpet and started sketching. "Let's win this."

CHAPTER 17

KAREEM

Kareem joined Eleanora at the table in the farthest corner of the cafeteria. Ever since coming up with Eleem, they'd spent every free moment talking and texting about their first piece. Without even noticing, this table had become *their* table, just north of the cluster of popular kids and to the east of the artsy crowd.

For the first time in over two weeks, Kareem was famished. He was so hungry, he was even willing to try the yellow goopy food. He took a big bite, then spat it back out. "What is this stuff?"

Ellie was happily scooping the goop into her mouth. "Mac and cheese! The best stuff on earth!"

"No." Kareem shook his head. "Americans did it right with hamburgers, fries, and milk shakes. This mac and cheese, I do not think so."

"What? How can you not like this creamy, heavenly goodness?"

Kareem felt so much better when he was around Ellie. He was still angry to be in Allansdale and with his parents for sending him away, and he desperately missed his friends. But somehow, this blue-banged girl made it all a little more tolerable.

Kareem pulled his notebook toward him. Sam was glancing over at their table. When their eyes met, she turned away quickly. When she'd introduced herself, Ellie had called Sam her best friend, but they didn't sit together or talk at school. In fact, he hadn't seen them say a word to each other since he arrived in Allansdale.

"Ellie, I have a question," he asked. He didn't like to pry, but after his fight with Sam, he needed to know. "Why aren't you talking to Sam? Are you two in a fight?"

Ellie's face dropped. Kareem felt like he had dumped a bucket of ice cubes onto her perfect, sizzling fire.

"I'm sorry," said Kareem. He didn't want to make her feel bad. "It's okay if you don't want to talk about it. It's just that I got in an argument with her the other day. So I was wondering . . ."

Ellie motioned toward Sam's table with her eyes.

"It's because of who she's sitting with," said Ellie. "She wants to be friends with someone who's a world-class jerk."

"But why does she want to be friends with those people so much?" Kareem asked.

"I don't know, Kareem. I guess she has always wanted to be part of the popular crowd." Ellie grabbed an apple, then seemed to think about his question a little more. "It's not just that. Sam always sees the good in people. Even after what happened to her, she still doesn't think Cat's that bad. She thinks she's changed. And you wouldn't believe what she did to her in fourth grade, Kareem. And all through fifth grade!"

Kareem's eyes widened as Ellie told him the whole history between Cat and Sam, and how Cat's bullying and nasty rumor-spreading had encouraged other kids to be unkind—like the kid who asked her if she owned camels as pets, or the one who'd said her father looked like Osama bin Laden. He felt a little pang of guilt, thinking about how Sam had told him he didn't know what it was like being the only Muslim, Arab kid in the school.

"I just don't know why she's determined to join this club," said Ellie despondently. "She thinks Spirit Squad is about more than Cat. But it's Cat's club. It'll always be her club."

Kareem nodded. He knew people like Cat back in Syria.

Ellie scooted closer to Kareem and handed him a notebook.

"Eleanora, I feel a little bad about Samira," said Kareem. "I didn't know any of this."

"Eventually she's going to figure out that Cat hasn't changed." She opened her notebook. "Come on. We have work to do."

They'd finally agreed on their first piece last night, after texting back and forth for nearly an hour. Ellie had wanted to do Kareem's chains with the Hamza hashtag, but Kareem said that one would give him away immediately.

"We just need people to wake up," he had texted. "To care."

"That's it!" Ellie had texted back.

They both knew they had it. They decided on: "Wake up. Look outside YOUR world!" Kareem had stayed up sketching ideas in his black book. Ellie had apparently done the same.

Kareem flipped through her drawings: an alarm clock ringing, a steaming coffee mug, a bear coming out of his cave, and a turtle peeking out of his shell.

He shifted in his seat. "I guess mine are a little darker."

He showed them to Eleanora: the earth on fire, a person taking off cracked glasses, and another ripping off an eye mask.

They left the two sketchbooks open, side by side.

"Okay, how about we somehow combine these?" said Ellie. "I like your earth and your eyes, but maybe they shouldn't be burning. Maybe something . . . I don't know . . . more positive?"

"Yes, you're right." Kareem fidgeted. He didn't quite know how to say this, so he was going to just spit it out. "Eleanora, I really like your drawings, but I don't want to use animals. And the coffee cup will make people think it's a Nescafé commercial. And nobody likes alarm clocks—you just want to shut those things up."

"Okay, I get it," said Ellie. "They don't work."

"You're a really good artist, Eleanora. I'm sorry. It's just—"

"It's okay, Kareem." She smiled. "I really do get it. I love my turtle, though. His name is Oscar."

"Right. Oscar." Kareem smiled back at her. "I like him, too."

He pushed his untouched tray aside. Ellie watched over his shoulder as he drew the Earth with a large, long-lashed eye looking out of the middle.

"How about this? Is this more *pos-i-tive?*"

"That's pretty cool," said Ellie, with a chuckle. "Yes, it's better."

They discussed how they could do it quickly. Kareem would make an Earth stencil from a cardboard box. They already had green, blue, black, and red spray chalk, and they researched how to make brown. When the bell rang, they agreed to meet at Eleanora's house after school to finalize the plan.

That evening, they blended blue and orange chalk in Ellie's kitchen to create the perfect shade of brown. They added corn starch and baking soda, before slowly drizzling in water. Once they nailed the consistency, they scooped it into a jar and sealed it shut.

Back home, Kareem made a globe stencil. He practiced drawing an eye with long, rich eyelashes, then tried spray-painting it with black spray chalk. He texted Eleanora pictures of his attempts, and she texted back the letters she created. When they were both happy, they decided on a location—a wall near city hall. It was highly visible, and tons of kids would pass it on their way to school. They'd leave at five a.m. Ellie said she'd use band as an excuse. It started later, but nobody would know what time she'd actually left. Kareem told his uncle he'd been invited to an early-morning soccer practice.

They were set.

Kareem opened the basement door and walked out into the dark, sleepy neighborhood. There wasn't a glimmer of light or a peep of sound as he waited outside Eleanora's house. It was so quiet, the crunch of leaves underfoot practically made him jump.

What was that?

He turned and flashed his flashlight. Some squirrels playing. He took a deep breath to calm himself. He hadn't been this pumped since he'd done his first piece with the boys. It didn't feel dangerous in the same way, but he was still excited.

Ellie quietly closed her front door and hurried over to join him.

Kareem laughed. "Really, all black? And isn't the hat a bit much?"

"Nope." Ellie's face was serious. "A beanie is not too much. We have a job to do."

Kareem laughed again. Between the all-black attire, an overstuffed backpack that looked like it might topple her, and her sparkly Converse, she was cat-burglar meets glitter anime.

"Yalla," said Ellie, obviously proud of her Arabic. "Hurry up. Move it!"

They walked through the brisk morning air, toward city hall. Ellie silently fidgeted with her backpack straps.

Kareem looked at her curiously. "Are you nervous? You seem nervous." He paused, then added, "You're . . . not talking."

"A little, I guess," she said. "I couldn't sleep last night, so I did an internet search and read that graffiti is illegal, even if it's washable."

"Really?" Compared to what he'd done in Syria, this was just fun. They were literally playing with chalk. For a second, he wondered what would happen if they got caught. Would his parents find out? What was that jail called? Jubey. But he thought about Hassan and the boys and confidently said, "I've never been caught. And I don't plan on getting caught here of all places."

Ellie smiled as she soaked up his confidence. "Yeah, I've never been caught, either."

Kareem laughed. "Right."

When they reached city hall, they got straight to work. Kareem started with the stencil, like they'd planned. He centered it on the wall with two good coats of green spray chalk. Meanwhile, Ellie worked on the lettering. Above the globe, she wrote in red: Wake up! Below: Look outside YOUR world.

Kareem filled in the Earth with blues and greens, then used the brown to create the eye and black to carefully spray curved eyelids, leaving the globe itself as the eyeball. With precise wrist flicks, he added long, dark lashes.

He checked his watch. "Six fifteen. Not bad."

They packed away their brushes and cans, then stood back to take it all in.

"Kareem, it's perfect," said Ellie. "People are gonna love it!"

This had been so easy, so effortless, compared to what Kareem had done in Syria. He wished Hassan, George, and Yusuf were with him. He took a picture with his phone, then texted Hassan.

Kareem

Hassan, guess what? I'm studying hard here too. But it's so much easier!

Hassan

WHAT? ARE YOU SERIOUS!

Kareem

Yep.

Kareem

Once a good student, always a good student.

Kareem wished he could say more. He put his phone away and ran to catch up with Ellie.

Yes, Kareem thought, as he admired the perfect, unmarked buildings on their way to school, *Allansdale is sure going to be surprised!*

CHAPTER 18

SAMIRA

Sam was supposed to wait for the other girls in the art room after school, but she started without them, drawing the long swishes of a lion's profile. She was so frustrated by Cat's declaration that the mascot had to be a part of their banner. They'd already done a lion.

To make it more interesting, Sam imagined a different type of lion. Determined and fierce, but also sleek and beautiful. Its teeth would be sharp, but not overly so. She wanted to play off the cat's natural confidence—her shiny coat, her mysterious gait, her wise face. Sam leaned in and focused on the eye, using two inverted brush sweeps to narrow it. At least she could make this one stunning.

She didn't have much time. The night before, her mom had given her yet another "who your friends are" lecture. Sam had heard it so many times, she could practically recite it by heart. Then her mom had directly asked if she was part of Spirit Squad. Again, Sam had fudged the truth by saying

Lucy, Avery, and Cat were, but that she was just helping with a project.

In the end, her mom gave her permission to stay at school to work on the project, with a strict five p.m. curfew. Sam would have to finish up by four to make it home in time.

As she drew the long lines of the lion's mane, she sensed someone behind her. She spun around and found Dylan standing right there, practically breathing down her neck.

"What are you doing?" she yelped. Embarrassed that he was so close, and that he was examining her work, she tried to obstruct his view of the lion with her body. "Get back to your side of the room!"

"Didn't know there were sides." Dylan grinned and ambled over to the water fountain outside. "I was just getting some water."

Amari was hunched over his phone at the soccer club's table across the room.

"Hey, Amari," Sam called. "Would you please stop your team from spying?" When he didn't respond, she yelled, "Hell-looooo? Amari!"

Ms. Little, the art teacher, peeked into the classroom. "Friends, you all need to keep it down. We're having an art club meeting next door. If you can't, I'm going to have to ask you all to leave."

"Sorry, Ms. Little," the group chimed.

Amari looked over at Sam and smirked once Ms. Little had left.

"What's up?" he whispered loudly. He held out his phone. "Hey, did you see this? It's so cool!"

Sam went over to look.

"It was on the wall right outside city hall this morning."

Sam scrunched her face in confusion. "*Our* city hall? Someone graffitied it?"

"I'm pretty sure it's not permanent," Amari said.

Sam admired the beautiful wide eye with its long, lush eyelashes. She loved the way the artist had integrated the lines of the globe with the lines of the lashes. They were in total sync.

"Isn't it awesome?" said Amari. "I just shared it on Twitter and on our school's boards. I'm kind of surprised anyone in Allansdale would do something like this."

Sam nodded, smiling. "Yeah, do people here even know what graffiti is?"

"Seriously," said Amari.

"Everyone knows what graffiti is!" said Dylan, examining Sam's unattended banner as he slowly walked by with water in hand.

"SERIOUSLY?" Sam charged back to her own table just as Cat, Avery, and Lucy entered the room. She glared at Dylan. "Stop spying on our banner!"

"Tsk, tsk," said Amari with a huge grin. "You heard what Ms. Little said. Keep it down, people."

"Dylan!" Cat planted her hands on her hips.

"We're just messing with you guys," said Dylan. "Why would we care about your banner?"

Amari dusted off his shoulders and picked up his paintbrush. "Yeah, we don't need to cheat. We got this."

"Then your side should stay on your side of the room," said Lucy.

As they bickered, Sam watched Kareem and Ellie enter the room and make their way to the supply closet. They slowed ever so slightly when they passed Sam's table, looking at her banner with an air of . . . well, Sam wasn't quite sure. But she was pretty sure it wasn't good. She knew what Ellie thought of Spirit Squad, and she suspected Kareem would agree. And now, here they were, whispering like they'd known each other for ages.

Like Sam didn't even matter.

What are they doing here? Are they working on a banner, too?

Sam lowered her head to avoid eye contact. Kareem was *Sam's* cousin. Not only had he been a complete jerk to her, he'd now stolen her best friend?

"Sam, why is the 'We're Number 1' so small?" Cat crinkled her face in disapproval. "It's practically hidden. The letters need to be bigger, like we really mean it!"

Distracted, Sam said, "I wanted it to fit into the lion's mane."

Are they talking about me?

She thought of Ellie's words, "She's using you, Sam," and felt her face redden.

Kareem unrolled a long piece of paper and held it out for Ellie to cut with scissors. Then he rolled it into a tight cylinder and placed it under his arm. They stopped at Sam's table on their way back to the main door.

"Hi, Samira," said Kareem, trying to make eye contact with her.

"How's it going?" Ellie asked her softly.

"Good," said Sam, her tone curt. Then she turned to Cat, who was still complaining about her lettering, as if Kareem and Ellie weren't even there. Sam barely heard her, but she nodded along. Why would Ellie show up here, with her cousin, after not speaking to her for almost three weeks? Ellie knew this was where Spirit Squad met after school. Were they trying to rub their friendship in her face? She just needed them to leave. Now.

"I'll see you at home, Samira," Kareem said.

Sam nodded, still avoiding his eyes. She could hear her heart pounding in her ears.

"Excuse me." Cat rolled her eyes at them. "Sam is busy." Then she pivoted back to Sam. "All this has to change," she barked, pointing to the top of the banner. "It's just all wrong!"

Sam flipped her hair and grabbed a pencil to redraw the lion's mane.

"Okaaaay," said Ellie, taking a deep breath and flaring her nostrils at Cat. Sam could tell that Ellie wanted to punch her.

Then, she patted Sam on the back and said, "Sam, she's wrong. Your letters are perfect."

Cat and Ellie stared at each other in silence.

"Okay, we have to go," said Kareem, pulling Ellie toward the door. "See you later, Samira."

Sam suddenly wanted to run after Ellie, give her a hug, and say she was sorry. Instead, she pretended to refocus on her drawing, and softly said "bye" under her breath. Once they'd gone, she put her head in her hands and let out a big sigh.

"Ellie has no idea what she's talking about," said Cat. "Those letters are all wrong."

"Cat, what are you talking about?" said Amari. He had crossed the room and was looking over her shoulder. "This looks great!"

Sam glanced at Cat, who was staring at her with narrowed eyes, like a lion eyeing its prey. Her letters were sharp and dagger-like. Sam rubbed her arm and suddenly wished her letters were invisible.

"It's just . . . it's just . . . ARGH. It's terrible!" Cat grabbed her bag and bolted out of the art room.

Sam just stood there with her pencil in hand, stunned.

"Umm, okay, Cat is really taking this banner competition seriously, isn't she?" said Amari.

"Yeah, my sis takes everything seriously," Dylan said. "But we're good now. Only the coolest people in the school are left."

"Wait, but you're still here?" Amari laughed, sauntering back toward Dylan, who punched him in the arm. "I guess you're cool because you hang with me," said Amari, playfully punching him back.

Sam giggled, their banter defusing the tension and confusion of the last few minutes. The two boys were so different, but they'd been friends for years—Sam assumed they'd bonded over soccer. Amari loved puncturing Dylan's know-it-all cockiness, but he somehow kept it playful, not mean. And no matter how much Dylan tried to dish it back, Amari always had the last laugh. Nobody else teased Dylan like that, but Dylan must like it, or he wouldn't keep hanging out with Amari.

Sam wished she was more comfortable around Dylan, instead of always feeling like a freak. Why could she talk to Amari so easily, but stumble and stammer and stutter whenever she tried talking to Dylan? Just as she was thinking about it, Dylan looked over and smiled at her.

Did that really just happen? Maybe he does like me?

Amari also turned toward her table, and made a two-fingered "I see you" gesture.

Sam smirked, then looked down at the banner, suddenly embarrassed.

Are they both flirting with me? Get a grip, Samira Sukkari. You're getting too into yourself.

She glanced at the clock. *Oh no.* It was already four thirty. She frantically gathered her things. "I'm late. See you all tomorrow."

The whole way home, Sam thought about Dylan and Amari, Cat, and Ellie and Kareem. Her worlds were jumbled. Out of sync.

She picked up her pace. All she knew for sure was that it would be really bad if she wasn't home by five.

◊

She burst in the front door a few minutes late, ready with her excuses and apologies, but her parents didn't even seem to notice. She found them in front of the TV, concentrating intently. An Arabic news ticker ran from right to left along the bottom of the screen, below a scene of young people yelling and running, panicked.

"Is this in Syria?" asked Sam, taking a seat in the armchair. Her mom nodded.

The perfectly coiffed newscaster was speaking in fancier, more formal Arabic than Sam was used to. She tried to read the ticker, but she didn't know all the words. The images were frantic. Scary. "What's happening?"

"They're protesting near Farah and Aziz's hospital today." Her dad made a *tsk tsk* sound while shaking his head. "The government forces fired back. A lot of people were killed and injured. It's starting."

Sam looked at the television, then back at her parents. Her mother's eyes were red, like she'd been crying. Her father sat on the edge of the couch, holding his chin in his hand, his eyes unblinking.

"What's starting?

"The crackdown. The government won't let people protest for too long."

"What do you mean?"

She knew her parents wouldn't tell her much. They always tried to "protect" her from all the bad news. She'd begun to realize they did it because they couldn't handle the news themselves. It made them too sad.

Her heart sank, thinking of Kareem's parents. "What about Amo Aziz and Tant Farah?"

"I don't know, habibti," said her mom. "They're needed there right now. Insha'Allah khair."

"Allah yustor," said her father.

Sam didn't exactly know what those terms meant, but she knew they weren't good-news expressions.

"I'll call them." Her dad stood and went to make the phone call from another room.

An hour ago, Sam had been so angry with Kareem, but now that seemed childish. She knew his parents had sent him away, but she'd never really asked why. Her parents had said he was in some sort of trouble, but they hadn't given her any specifics, and it hadn't occurred to her that things could get worse in Syria. Now it was obvious that his parents were right in the middle of something really dangerous. How would she feel if she found out from the TV news that her parents were a mile away from gunfire and violence? Kareem must be so scared and worried. Guilt and sadness and anxiety swirled together inside her. She had to talk to him—she had to try again.

CHAPTER 19

KAREEM

Kareem grabbed his soccer ball and backpack, slammed his locker shut, and walked out of the school with Ellie.

"Check it out!" Ellie handed him her phone. "Amari put our piece on the school's social media board! And look what he wrote."

My New Heroes. Whoever They Are.
#AllansdaleGraffitiRocks #GraffitiGangHeroes

Graffiti heroes. Kareem liked the sound of that. Maybe he could do something that mattered in this little town?

"This is great!" said Ellie. "Amari is one of the most popular boys in school. If he shares it, everybody else will, too." She took her phone back. "See? It's already been shared by forty-six people. And liked two hundred times. Not bad, huh?"

"Not bad," Kareem repeated, dribbling the ball ahead of him. He thought about how easy it had been. The graffiti,

148

taking the picture, walking to school afterward. And now walking home and talking about it, all out in the open. "You know, if I had done that with Hassan and my other friends in Syria, we would have needed two lookouts. And an escape plan."

Ellie smiled. "I had an escape plan prepared. I was gonna kick them in the shin so you could get away and then I'd run after you."

"Great, Eleanora," said Kareem, laughing. "That's great."

"I know."

Kareem bounced the ball on his knee before gently bringing it to the ground using the front of his foot.

"Hey, you're good at that," said Ellie. "Maybe you should try out for a soccer team? There are really good club teams around here, too."

"No, I am not interested."

"Why not? You're as good as the best players. Maybe better."

Kareem shook his head and worked on another trick. "Eleanora, I'm just here for a few weeks."

"I know," said Ellie. "I mean, just in case you stay a little longer."

"I won't. I'm going home." He could tell he had upset her, but he needed to be honest. There was no sense in getting her hopes up that he might stay. Anyway, his soccer buddies were back home—he definitely wasn't joining a team in America.

They walked on in silence.

"Kareem, what was it like? Being in Syria?"

Kareem stopped the ball with his foot and looked at Ellie. He loved that she was so curious about where he was from. Somehow it made him feel more welcome.

"It was good—and bad—and good."

He explained how much he loved Syria and Damascus and how one day, she'd have to visit him there. He described his idyllic life. How he lived for soccer and hanging out with his friends, how they went out for sandwiches after every game on the weekends. He told her about Hassan and George and Yusuf. How George was an amazing soccer player, how Yusuf loved to play tricks, and how Hassan had been his best friend since he was five.

"Actually, you remind me of Hassan." He glanced at her sideways. "He's funny. A little different. I think if his mom let him, he'd have blue hair, too. But he . . . he follows the rules too much."

"A quirky rule follower," Ellie said, smiling. "Yeah, I'm sort of like that."

"Right," said Kareem. "He's kirky."

She let out a huge laugh. "No, *quirky*. Like KWAH. KWIR-key. It rhymes with Turkey."

"Yes, you are definitely a turkey." Then he turned serious again. "Another thing about living in Syria—people don't just talk about things publicly like they do here. They're too scared, because there are informants everywhere. So we don't discuss the government or politics outside of our homes."

She was listening, so he kept talking. He told her how people worked hard, but sometimes it didn't matter because there was so much corruption. And then he described the boys from Dara'a, and the graffiti, and the excitement of revolution.

"You could feel the change in the air." Kareem's steps got lighter. He picked up the ball and looked at Ellie. "It's like everybody decided, at the same time, that enough was enough."

"And this all happened because of the boys from Dara'a?"

"Not only because of them. But that was like . . . it's the spark that lit the match, you know? They went after kids. And it's not like they arrested one or two. It was fifteen!"

Ellie looked shaken. Kareem hadn't meant to upset her, but to understand the hopeful part, she first had to learn about the bad stuff. She'd never had to think about people, let alone young children, being arrested or tortured. But he appreciated that she cared. His own cousin hadn't bothered to ask him about his friends or what was happening at home. And Eleanora didn't need to say anything—it was written all over her face.

Kareem felt bad putting so much on her at once. He popped the ball up onto his neck, letting it roll down his back, to lighten the mood.

"Show-off," said Ellie, forcing a laugh. She slid in front of him and tried to steal the ball, but he swiped it behind him so she couldn't reach.

"Darn it," she said. "Almost got it."

"Right, almost," he teased.

They walked the rest of the way in silence. When they reached their street, Ellie said, "Want to come over? The food pantry's doing a donation drive. You could help me with the poster. Aaaand . . . I have an idea for a new piece!"

"Already?"

"I just thought of it while you were talking. How about: 'What if you were AFRAID to speak?'" she said. "Maybe if people here were afraid, we'd want to speak up more?"

Kareem grinned. It was good. She'd completely understood what he had been trying to explain to her.

"Eleanora, it's perfect. We could add 'Freedom is Everything!'"

Now all they needed was a drawing to go with the new tagline, and he already had ideas.

"I was thinking outside the library would be another good spot," said Ellie. "Maybe even tomorrow morning? You know, hit twice in two days!"

Kareem grinned. Eleanora had a wild look in her eyes; she was speaking faster with each word. His phone buzzed, and he took it out. It was an alert from one of the Arabic sites he'd signed on to so he could stay up-to-date with Syrian news.

PROTESTERS FIRED UPON IN FIVE CITIES ACROSS THE COUNTRY

Kareem's eyes widened. He opened Twitter and read through the Syria hashtags. Protests had been met with live fire. There were pictures from Homs, Hasakeh, Deir Az-Zor, Hama, smaller towns . . . and the outskirts of Damascus. Videos of panicked and injured protesters. People were running for their lives, and here he was, playing with chalk.

He texted his parents, then sent Hassan, Yusuf, George, and Ramy coded messages asking if they were okay.

Was Hassan there? I'm sure he didn't go. Yusuf probably went. Did they all go with Ramy?

"Eleanora, I have to go," said Kareem, curtly.

"Why? What happened?" asked Ellie. "Are you okay?"

"I am, but . . . I have to go."

He ran into his uncle's house, silently praying: *Ya Allah, let them be okay. Ya Rab, let them be okay.* He stopped at the living room's entrance. Samira, Tant Ranya, and Khalo Ahmed were watching the news. They all turned, wide-eyed, to look at him. The TV newscaster was mentioning the protests Kareem had just learned about. And then, news of an explosion. Kareem's heart raced. He hadn't read about any explosions.

He stood there, frozen, taking it all in.

"Habibi, I already talked to your mom. They are okay," his uncle said quickly. "They'll call later."

Kareem took a deep breath, letting the words sink in.

They're okay, they're okay.

"Kareem," said his uncle again. "Did you hear me? They're okay."

"Yes, Amo," said Kareem. "I heard you."

"Why don't you join us, habibi?" his uncle said, motioning to Samira to make space between them. He tapped the empty spot next to him. "Right here."

Kareem didn't want to sit. He didn't want sympathy. He didn't want to hear their commentary or worries or deal with any questions. All he wanted was his mom. But she wasn't there. These weren't his parents. They weren't his friends. He never asked to be here.

He slowly walked over and squeezed himself in the small space between his uncle and cousin on the couch. Kareem's shoulders pressed up against Sam's as his uncle's long legs forced him to move even farther over into Sam's space. His aunt Ranya sat on the loveseat next to them.

They watched Al Jazeera in silence.

"Kareem, they're going to be okay," said Samira, still looking at the television. "They're going to be fine."

Nobody could predict the future. He knew Samira was just trying to make him feel better. But he felt like the room's walls were closing in on him and that the air in the room had thinned.

"Insha'Allah," he mumbled, breathing in deeply.

"I think we've seen enough," said his Khalo Ahmed. "We know they're safe. There's no point in watching this on repeat. Yalla, let's eat."

After dinner, Kareem excused himself and ran straight to his room. He lay on his bed and checked his messages. Still no response from his friends. His eyes clouded with tears. He thought of that first protest they'd attended together, and how happy they'd been. And his mom's words: *The government won't let this go on for too long. It's only a matter of time.*

Ramy had told them if the protesters showed up, they would win. There was no alternative. The protesters were in the right, so they had to prevail.

At eleven, his phone pinged, but it was just Eleanora.

Ellie

> Here it is. Freedom is EVERYTHING. What if you were AFRAID to speak?

Ellie

> What drawing did you come up with?

Kareem thought about their newest idea. It was . . . exactly right. Look at his friends. They weren't allowed to protest, but they dared to speak up, and now he was worried sick. He picked up his notebook and started sketching. He drew protesters holding signs and a boot coming down to crush them. He turned to a fresh page. A group of girls whispering to one another, looking over their shoulders. No, too discreet.

It was nearly two a.m. Somehow, he'd been drawing for hours. He picked up his phone and checked the news, blearily imagining a headline like "Hassan is okay" or "George is home playing soccer."

He turned off his light. Then his phone vibrated again, lighting up the room. HASSAN!

Hassan

> Mneeh. I'm here, habibi. I didn't answer because I was sleeping!

Hassan

> Mom took away my phone yesterday so I couldn't go.

Hassan

> But we're okay. Everybody is okay. Alhamdulillah. ☺

Kareem called him. It was good to hear his voice. Kareem asked about the "news" and Hassan wavered. Kareem knew Hassan couldn't say much over the phone, but he understood from the hints.

"The party was fun," Hassan said. "I didn't go, but Yusuf and Ramy did."

Relief washed over Kareem. So Hassan hadn't gone to the protest, but Yusuf and Ramy had. Everybody was all right. That was what mattered.

They chatted for a while about soccer and how Kareem was "studying" with Ellie. When Kareem hung up, he said a little prayer, thanking God for keeping his friends safe. He wondered how much Hassan had actually wanted to attend the protest. Kareem couldn't quite tell from their call, and he couldn't just ask him straight up. He missed Hassan. A lot. And he hated waiting to hear from him.

Kareem switched the lights back on and grabbed his notebook. They needed something simpler. He drew open red lips with a circle and line that went right through them. He smiled. That was it. Easy to execute, but clear and to the point.

He looked at his alarm clock. Four a.m. He got dressed and grabbed the backpack of spray chalk. It was early enough that they could do this without getting caught. Adrenaline surged through his body as he quietly opened the back door, crossed the dark street, and tapped on Ellie's window.

"Wake up!" he whispered loudly. "Let's go, *Che-Ellie Guevara.*"

CHAPTER 20

SAMĪRA

Sam tapped on Kareem's door and loudly whispered, "Kareem? Are you awake?"

No answer. She gently pushed the door open and stepped inside. "Kareem?"

It was seven in the morning, but Kareem was gone. His bedroom looked like a bare hotel room. His bed was already made. Textbooks were neatly stacked on the desk. Sam opened his math book and felt the spine crack.

Has he even used them?

Come to think of it, she'd never seen him study, or heard him mention school. His closet was wide open. The hangers were empty, but clothes spilled out of his suitcase on the floor. He hadn't even unpacked.

Sam twirled her hair. Where was he?

A large roll of paper was propped against the wall in the corner of the room. She knew she shouldn't look. But she couldn't help herself. Curious, she unrolled it.

It was a picture of a mouth inside a circle, with a red slash going through it. FREEDOM IS EVERYTHING. WHAT IF YOU WERE AFRAID TO SPEAK? At the bottom was written: #SPEAKUP #FREEDOM.

It had been colored with oil pastels. She flipped to the next sheet, and her jaw dropped. It was the piece Amari had posted yesterday. "Look Outside Your World! Wake up!"

Sam gasped.

Oh. My. God. Kareem's the graffiti artist.

She thought of Kareem and Ellie looking through the art cupboard together. Is this what they'd been doing?

Ellie's a part of this?

Sam let the papers fall to the floor. Her cousin—who had come from Syria just a few weeks ago, and was nearly mute around her family, and had humiliated her in front of her friends— was doing graffiti in small, sleepy, mind-your-own-business Allansdale. *With her best friend!* She didn't know whether to be impressed or furious or proud. How had she missed the signs? Kareem lived with her! How had this all started? How had he and Ellie become friends in the first place? She had so many questions.

Sam heard her mom's voice upstairs. She put the rolled papers back in the corner of the room, pulled Kareem's door shut, and ran up to breakfast.

"Samira, wein Kareem?" asked her mom as she got ready for work.

"I think he left for school already." She slung her backpack over her shoulder. "Mom, I gotta go. I have to study for my math quiz before class."

Sam walked as quickly as she could to school, her mind racing. She hoped she'd be able to find Kareem before the first bell.

As she neared the school, she noticed walls and rocks and fence posts tagged with **#SPEAKUP #GODEEPER #WAKEUP! #LookOutsideYourWorld.** Outside the library, in bright, big, bold red letters, was the exact piece she had just seen in Kareem's room: **FREEDOM IS EVERYTHING. WHAT IF YOU WERE AFRAID TO SPEAK?** Sam stood in front of it, stunned.

They tagged the building right next to school. That takes guts.

"I just shared it on social media." Amari appeared beside her. "It's pretty awesome."

Sam couldn't help smiling. "Yeah, it really is."

"I just want to know who's doing this?" asked Amari.

"No idea," she said quietly.

Other students gathered around them, talking loudly about the piece. Sam and Amari stood in silence.

"Hey, Amari. Hey, Sam." Dylan arrived with Cat trailing right behind. "Did you see it? I can't believe they did this right outside our school."

"Oh my God, are you kidding?" Cat stomped around her brother. "You like this?"

"What's not to like?" exclaimed Amari. In a teasing tone, he added, "Actually, maybe you should take it as advice, Cat. What if *you* were afraid to speak? People would be nicer to you."

"Ha-ha-ha." Cat planted her hands on her hips. "I can't believe you're both okay with *vandalism!*"

"It's called street art, Cat," said Amari. "It's saying something. Plus, it's not permanent. I'm not sure what they used, but I touched it yesterday and it came off on my fingers."

"I think it's spray chalk," Dylan said. "It'll be gone by the next rain."

"It doesn't matter if it's permanent or not," Cat snapped. "This is how it starts. First it's spray chalk, then it's chalk mixed with paint, and then it's full-on graffiti. Our parents were talking about it last night. Things like this always start small. The next thing you know, your whole town looks like . . . like . . . you know, the ghetto."

"The ghetto?" Amari raised his eyebrows. "Alert the authorities, Cat Spencer! Someone played with chalk."

Cat's face went red, and she turned and stormed off toward the school's entrance.

Sam examined the words again. The letters were rushed, slanted, and all the same size. They probably didn't have a lot of time, but she would have made the word "afraid" larger, in all caps, and smeared the paint so that it looked like brushstrokes that imparted fear. And then she would have made the word "freedom" flow, like it was a stream that needed to wash over the fear. Her heart started to beat faster. She needed to be a part of this. She had a role to play.

"Y'all, Cat's already started." Amari laughed and held up his phone. "Check out the school's boards."

"But she literally just left," said Sam, confused. She opened her feed. Sure enough, Cat had posted the newest piece with the hashtags: #NotArt #Vandalism #KeepOurStreetsClean! #ProtectPublicProperty

"Oh my God, she's so annoying!" Dylan groaned. "Why does she have to be MY sister?"

"She's definitely flipping out over this," said Amari.

"I'd better go," said Sam. "The bell's about to ring."

She hurried into school, wondering where Kareem and Ellie could be. On her way to the seventh-grade lockers, she saw Cat whispering to Avery, Tom, and a few other Spirit Squad members in the hallway. Her face was still flushed.

"Sam! Wait up!"

She turned around and found Dylan running after her, breathless.

"Hey, I was wondering, do you want to come by this weekend?" he asked.

Sam blinked at him, confused. Was Dylan inviting her over to his house? By herself?

"I mean, I'm having another party this weekend."

"Oh yeah, sure," she said, flustered. "Well, I have to check. I'll let you know. I'm still sort of grounded. I think." She was babbling again. The bell blared, rescuing her from the awkward moment. "Gotta go! Late for class!" She bolted up the stairwell and into the girls' bathroom.

Sam

LAYLA! NEED TO TALK! EMERGENCY!

Sam

Kareem and Ellie have been graffitiing Allansdale.

Sam

And it's SO GOOD. I have no idea how this even happened!

Sam

And Cat's tweeting about how it's vandalism. Knowing her, she's totally going to make a big deal about it all. She's STILL so annoying!

Sam

And Dylan just asked me to another party!

She paused and thought about Amari and how much he loved the graffiti and how he had stood up to Cat. Nobody intimidated him. Her stomach tingled.

Sam

And . . . I might have a crush on two boys!

Sam

WHERE ARE YOU? HELP!

CHAPTER 21

KAREEM

Kareem waited for Eleanora at their table in the cafeteria. This morning, they had executed their best piece yet. It had been riskier since it was closer to school, but they'd done it in fifteen minutes flat. When they finished, Ellie and Kareem took a selfie in front of it.

All morning, he couldn't stop thinking about what it would feel like to do this one with his friends in Syria. It would've worked there, too. Except they wouldn't need the second part: *What if you were afraid to speak?* They already knew what that felt like.

"Kareem, we're famous!" Ellie sat down across from him. "I mean, we're popular . . . you know, if anyone knew it was us. Which they don't."

Kareem chuckled. "Yes, *we* are the popular unpopular ones."

Together, they scrolled through the tweets and the school's boards. Although Kareem hated to admit it, he liked having so many people pay attention to their small act of resistance. But something still felt off.

"Do you think it'll make a difference?" he asked. "Will it make people think?"

"I don't know. Probably not." Ellie paused. "Then again, they're reading it before they retweet it." She scrolled through more posts, then suddenly stopped. Her eyes bulged. "Umm, we have a little problem."

"Did someone get a picture of us?"

"No, it's not that." Ellie's knee started to bounce. "It's Cat Spencer." She pushed the phone toward Kareem.

He rolled his eyes. Cat had posted a picture of a dirty alleyway with trash everywhere. "Graffiti Is Vandalism. Period." #NotArt #GraffitiIsVandalism

"It's being retweeted," Ellie said. "There's, like, thirty retweets already! Half the Spirit Squad has shared it!"

Kareem shrugged. "Does that mean our minute of popularity is over?"

"Um, might be." Her eyes were wide beneath her bright blue bangs. "She says that if the vandals are students, they should be expelled!"

"Expelled, right. It's chalk, Ellie. They need to calm down."

"Kareem, you don't understand. She's the most popular girl in school. And her parents own, like, half the town." Ellie rubbed her forehead and pursed her lips tight.

Kareem didn't like seeing her this upset. He wished he could reassure her. Why was Samira hanging out with this rude

Cat Spencer? And why would the most popular girl in school care about a bit of graffiti chalk? It was completely absurd.

Wait. Cat was the most popular girl in school.

A calm came over Kareem, and his eyes lit up. "Ellie, our path to fame is just starting. This is a *good* thing." He grabbed his sketchbook. "I have an idea."

His hand moved across the page so quickly, he wasn't even sure what he was drawing. But he knew it was right. "People here are a little clueless. They have so much, they don't even know what they have."

Ellie swiped her bangs away to get a better view of what he was doing. "How is this good, Kareem? It definitely feels bad."

Kareem tried to explain as he worked. He finally had the answer to a question he'd been asking himself since he arrived. "This is why we need to do graffiti here, Eleanora. Because people . . . people . . ."

The words and the drawing were competing for space in his head, and he couldn't push them both out at the same time. Instead, he silently finished the drawing and angled it to show Ellie. "People here don't even think about freedom. We're going to make them think about it. Sometimes, to get a message across, all you need is a little controversy. And Cat's giving that to us."

He had drawn a young boy protesting, alone, holding a sign. On the sign, Kareem had written: What Is Spirit Anyway? A Free Spirit Needs Freedom of Speech!

"Oh, I get it," said Ellie, perking up. "We can counterattack! We'll bring Spirit Squad down!"

Kareem's eyes widened. "Is that really our goal?"

"Well, no . . . but if anybody is clueless about *spirit* and freedom, it's that stupid squad! And everybody follows them!"

"Okay—we're not attacking them, but we can use Spirit Squad to get some attention."

A smile appeared on Ellie's face. "Okay, fine. I'm down with that." She smiled wider. "Can we attack a little, though? Please? Like a mini-attack. You know, not like a full-on offensive. Like . . . why is there no word for 'mini-attack'?"

Kareem laughed.

"I have an idea," said Ellie, jumping up in excitement. "We need to infiltrate the school with this one. You know, so that we pound . . . umm, I mean, *reach* Spirit Squad. What if we make stickers and put them all over school? I mean, we could also do a chalk drawing somewhere too, but we need to get the message *inside* the school. And we'd put them everywhere. You know, make it look like a giant sneezed graffiti stickers."

"I don't know," said Kareem, looking at Eleanora dubiously. "I'm not into stickers. We're supposed to be doing graffiti."

"It'll be easy, Kareem. And it'll work. We can start with the bathrooms, and then the classrooms, and whenever we walk, we can have them in our hands, ready to stick. We'll be like spies planting bugs under tables. But it'll be on top of the tables, of course. I mean, nobody would see them if we put them under tables. Unless they dropped their pencil or something. We could put them on whiteboards and classroom doors and bulletin boards. It'll be so fun. And dangerous. Undercover graffiti sticker artists. And my dad has packs of stickers he uses for public service announcements for the police station. And they peel off easily, so we won't ruin anything. I can even print them tonight, when my dad is asleep."

Kareem smiled. This girl could talk. Sometimes his head spun trying to keep up with her. But he loved that Eleanora understood him. And she was right. The point was to get the message across. Even if it was with a little flair . . . or stickers. He turned his mind to colors and execution. Everybody was okay back home, and he had Eleanora with him. For now, it was enough.

CHAPTER 22

KAREEM

"Hey, slow down!" yelled Kareem, stopping beside the high wall at the park's entrance. "How about this wall?"

Ellie turned back and frowned. "Isn't it too exposed?"

A few days earlier, they'd done their "What Is Spirit Anyway?" sticker campaign. It had gone perfectly. They'd executed their bright chalk drawing just across the street from the school, and then they'd placed the matching stickers *everywhere*. Like Ellie had suggested, they started with the bathrooms and then managed to get the stickers into almost every classroom, avoiding the main hallway because of the cameras. Ellie had narrowly escaped getting caught by the janitor in the morning and Kareem had had to pretend to study for a math test during third period, when a seventh-grade math teacher appeared from out of nowhere in the art room. They estimated they had placed a hundred stickers before the morning announcement, and another fifty by lunch. By nine a.m., Amari had shared the chalk piece. Then Cat had lost her mind on Twitter and on the school boards. She took it as a full-on assault and started a social media campaign of her own: #SpiritIsEverything #StopPollutingOurTown #NOStickers #NOGraffiti.

At lunch, Ellie and Kareem kept mouthing *no stickers!* at each other and then collapsing into giggles.

By dismissal, the entire school was in an uproar, talking about their spirit graffiti. Opinions were evenly divided—half siding with Amari and Dylan, and the rest agreeing with Cat and the Spirit Squad. The only person who seemed oddly silent was his own cousin. But Kareem wasn't surprised—Samira never seemed to stand for anything.

Ellie and Kareem had decided to keep the momentum going. The park's front wall was perfect.

"Okay, you're good," Ellie said, taking the first turn as lookout. "All clear."

Kareem sprayed, high on the wall's entrance: #FREEDOMIS-EVERYTHING! #USEIT

Ellie went next, writing: GRAFFITI IS ACTIVISM, NOT VANDALISM. She reached for a can of blue spray chalk and said mischievously, "Something about Spirit again? How about 'Freedom Is *Our* Spirit'?"

Kareem nodded, and she tagged the cement ground at the entrance.

"You know, maybe we should do a piece about . . ." Ellie paused for a minute to think. "Animal cruelty? Or global warming. Our school doesn't even recycle! Or maybe . . . homelessness.

There are guys who sleep in the park. I met them when I volunteer at the soup kitchen with my dad. Nobody here even notices them." Ellie looked sad. "It's like they're invisi—"

Kareem heard the rustle of leaves. He scanned his surroundings.

Maybe an animal.

"Yes, yes," he said in a hushed whisper. "Eleanora, stop talking and hurry up."

"I'm just going to add one more, up here." Ellie had climbed halfway up the wall. "I'm almost done. I mean, it's like nobody sees them. Everybody deserves to be seen, Kareem."

Ya Allah, what is she talking about?

Kareem turned to scan both sides of the street. From the northern end, he spotted a police officer turning the corner, on foot.

"The police!" Kareem grabbed the backpack full of cans and tugged on Ellie's arm. "Let's go. Out! Out!"

Ellie jumped down and they took off through the gate's large archway, running as fast as they could.

"Hurry, Ellie," yelled Kareem. He didn't know the park that well and Ellie wasn't that fast.

He looked behind them and thought he heard footsteps. The officer must have seen their work and started chasing them.

"This way, Kareem." Ellie pushed her way through a hedge to an entirely different path. Within a few minutes, they had made it clear to the other side of the park.

Ellie slowed down and led Kareem to another path, this one larger. In the distance, they spotted a group of kids playing soccer.

"We can blend in," said Ellie.

Kareem's eyes lit up. Yes, he could join the soccer game. That would be great cover.

Someone called their names, and they ran toward the field.

"Kareem! Ellie! Over here!"

Amari was waving at them.

"You guys want to play?" Amari was wearing crimson shorts and a Liverpool jersey.

A group of kids were playing soccer, while Lucy, Sam, and Tom sat at nearby picnic tables, chatting.

"Man, we don't need more players," Dylan whispered loudly to Amari.

Amari waved him away. "Sure we do. I've seen Kareem handle a ball outside the school. He's good."

"He is!" Sam called. "I've seen videos of his games. He'll kick your butts."

"Yeah, I'll play." Kareem took off his sweatshirt and dropped it on the sideline. He glanced over at Ellie, raising his eyebrows.

"He's great," Ellie said, still scanning the path behind them for any signs that they had been followed. "Soccer's not my thing. I'd kick your butts in basketball. I'm out. Kareem, on the other hand . . ." She joined Sam and the others on the sideline.

"Go AMS!" Sam cheered.

Amari kicked the ball to Kareem. The ball felt good at Kareem's feet, especially on the soft grass. He bounced it off his knees and then juggled it back and forth between his feet. Then he lobbed it into the air and headed it.

"Show-off," Amari said with a smile. "See, Dylan? Told you he's good. Come on, let's go!"

The AMS team was Amari, Dylan, and some other kids Kareem recognized, but didn't know. Their opponents were older, maybe high school students. Kareem hadn't seen any of them before.

Kareem threw in the ball to start the game. He ran down the field, the breeze on his face. He intercepted the ball, dribbled around two defenders, then kicked it into the top right-hand corner of the net.

"GOAL!" yelled Dylan. The spectators exploded into cheers.

It had been a long time since Kareem had played. He loved running in the spring air with a ball at his feet. After almost an hour, he was gasping. He headed to the sideline for some water, and stopped hesitantly near Sam. He shot Eleanora a questioning look—she and Sam were sitting together, and it looked like they might have been talking.

His phone pinged. He'd heard it a few times while he was playing, but he'd been having too much fun to stop and check it. He fumbled it open, suddenly frightened. *What if something happened back home? How could I ignore my phone like that?*

Hassan

> I have a big test tomorrow. Studying so hard. Going to ace it.

Hassan

> You're gonna be so proud.

Kareem opened Hassan's ShamGram Twitter account. Hassan had posted a picture of a pro-regime slogan with an X over it: "Assad or We'll Burn the Country."

"The shabiha," Kareem mumbled. Regime thugs were counter-graffitiing. Interesting. Below Hassan's post was another one. Just words. In bold black and red letters.

FREEDOM REQUIRES NO PERMISSION! FREE SYRIA.

Then the hashtags:

#WeAreAllHamza

#FreedomNOW

#SprayMan

Kareem froze. Spray Man again. Was Hassan working with him? Suddenly it dawned on him . . . he was almost sure of it. He had no proof. But, deep down, he knew it. Ramy was Spray Man, the most famous graffiti artist in Syria. And Hassan and his friends were his graffiti gang. In just a few weeks, the hashtag Spray Man had appeared out of nowhere and become a household name in the Twitter-sphere. Kareem had wondered if Ramy was part of Spray Man's gang. But now, he was pretty sure that Ramy *was* Spray Man.

In the end, his identity didn't matter. He had inspired them to join the artistic revolution. It looked like Hassan was full-on in. He was going to do it. Maybe tomorrow? Kareem's heart raced.

What's he thinking? This is too dangerous.

Kareem furiously typed a message.

Kareem

> You don't need to study anymore. Khalas. It's too hard. You need to sleep sometimes.

His throat tightened. *Please, please let him understand this.*

Hassan

> It's fine. I'm going to get a perfect score. You're going to love my #s. Gotta go.

Kareem

> Please. No. It's enough.
> You don't need to get all the #s right.

But Hassan had already gone.

He had wanted to type: *It's too dangerous. You'll get caught.* But that would be too obvious. If the mukhabarat seized Hassan's phone, it could be used as proof he had done it. This was all Kareem's fault. When he was in Syria, he was the one pushing Hassan to use the hashtag, but that was before the gunfire and the explosions and the violence had really spread. From the outside, it seemed so much more dangerous. Was it really getting worse? It had always been unsafe. Kareem knew that. But from so far away, he could too easily imagine bad things happening to his friends. The risk no longer felt worth it. They were his best friends in the world, and he needed them to be okay. Kareem looked at the laughing faces around him. What was he doing here? He put his phone away and grabbed his sweatshirt.

"Hey, where're you going?" Amari called.

"Kareem?" Ellie asked. "What's wrong?"

"I have to go," Kareem said, waving his arm. "Thanks."

Kareem walked quickly toward the park's exit. He glanced back and saw Eleanora following him. He started to run, picking up speed. He needed to be alone, to create space between him and everybody else. Including Eleanora. He had to somehow convince Hassan not to do that piece—it was just too dangerous. And nobody here would understand.

CHAPTER 23

SAMIRA

Her heart sinking, Sam watched Kareem and Ellie disappear from view. For once, it had seemed like Kareem was having a great time. Sam had finally caught a glimpse of the same kid who'd gone to Disneyland with her years ago. But then he checked his phone and his mood changed completely. What happened? Sam jumped up and stuffed her things into her bag.

"Sam, are you okay?" asked Lucy.

"I need to go." Sam fumbled with her sweater. "I need to check on Kareem."

The last half hour had been too good to be true. Everything had finally come together, the jumbled pieces of her life sliding into place to form a picture of momentary happiness. Ellie had sat with them, and she'd even talked to Lucy a bit. Kareem was enjoying himself. Cat wasn't there. For the first time in weeks, things were . . . easy.

Kareem had been a series of harsh, black, unreadable scribbles ever since he'd arrived in Allansdale. But in the last thirty minutes, Sam had clearly seen his letters—fast, confident, flowing, strident Arabic. They mirrored the way he played soccer: graceful, but fast and aggressive. Mostly, he played soccer much like everyone else on the field: just a kid who wanted to score goals.

Until he checked his phone.

Sam headed for the park's main gate, slowing when she saw the fresh graffiti.

#FreedomIsEverything! #UseIt. Graffiti Is Activism, NOT Vandalism.

She had to admit it was good. But her stomach churned when she read the rest.

#FreedomIsOurSpirit.

Come on. Couldn't they just say what they had to say without poking at Spirit Squad?

Sam kept moving, picking up speed. Had something happened to Tant Farah or Amo? She thought about how Kareem had run down to his room when they were watching the news. How lonely it must be to worry about your family, your parents, and your friends all by yourself. That day, she'd decided to give him space. Her mom always said that Americans gave each other too much space. But her parents were different—they didn't even let Sam close the door to her own room. They joked that Arabs didn't believe in privacy.

Now, she wondered whether her mom had a point. Had she left him alone for his sake or her own? Maybe she'd only told herself she was giving Kareem space because she didn't want to get rejected again. Because it was hard. What he was going through was hard, and deep down, it made Sam uncomfortable. What if she'd abandoned him when what he really needed was for someone to be there for him? Sam didn't like to think about things that made her sad, mostly because she couldn't fix them. But now she prayed, for the first time, that her aunt and uncle were safe.

When she arrived home, Ellie was on the porch, staring at her phone.

"Is he okay?" Sam asked. "Why are you outside?"

"He won't let me in." Ellie's voice was strained.

Sam could always tell exactly how Ellie was feeling by looking into her eyes. Worry oozed out of them.

"Let me try." Sam unlocked the front door. "I'll call you after I talk to him. And . . . thank you, Ellie."

Ellie looked at Sam, confused.

"You know, for taking such good care of my cousin these last few weeks."

It's my turn to help him.

CHAPTER 24

KAREEM

Kareem sat on his bedroom floor and opened his sketchbook. Who had put Hassan up to this? This wasn't his style. Maybe Yusuf? Or even Ramy? Or could Hassan be doing this to prove something to him?

He texted everybody—Yusuf, George, Hassan, Ramy— hoping to find out more about Hassan, about the piece, about *anything*. He studied the picture again and scrolled through his Twitter feed, searching for more news.

@SyriaNews: Clashes erupt in Homs; Seven killed.

@SyriaRevolution: Funerals for fallen protesters met with live fire.

Kareem's stomach dropped. The security forces were firing on funeral processions? People couldn't even lay their dead to rest in peace. He retrieved his prayer rug from the closet. His mama had packed it for him and told him not to forget to pray, but this was the first time he'd bothered. Well, it was the first time he'd done it properly. He'd made du'as, asking God to protect his friends, but he'd stopped *praying* praying—five times a day, head to the floor, the way Muslims were supposed to.

After he finished, he sat on his prayer rug and made a du'a for his friends, asking Allah to protect them. Then he asked Allah to make the protesters invisible to the police, to keep them safe, to shield them from bullets.

As he placed his forehead on his mat, he choked up. The lowest point of prayer, the most vulnerable. He stayed in sujud. For the first time since his arrival in Allansdale, his entire body relaxed. There was so much he could not control. So much love, so much fear, so much longing—and it was all out of his hands. He felt he had been stripped of both clothes and skin; and yet, for a brief moment, a sudden quiet fell over him. He sat up, his eyes still closed. Then he exhaled, got up, grabbed his notebook, and started drawing. Three friends in a circle, tied together. Beside them, kids playing soccer on an open field.

A light knock, and his door opened. Sam was standing there in the doorway silently.

"Samira, what do you want?" he asked, his head in his hands.

"Are Tant Farah and Amo Aziz okay?" she asked. "Did something happen?"

Kareem raised his eyes. Samira seemed worried. Her own eyes were soft, as if she might cry.

"They're fine, Samira," he said, returning to his drawing.

Sam sat next to him and peered over his shoulder. Normally, he would have closed the sketchbook, but he didn't.

"I know you and Ellie are the graffiti artists," she said.

Kareem's hand stopped mid-stroke. "Are you going to turn us in?"

"Of course not."

Kareem put down his pencil. "If you did, I wouldn't care." What he and Eleanora did here didn't matter much, anyway. It's not like their lives were in danger. Not like Hassan's. Kareem's eyes welled with tears, so he closed them until they dried. When he reopened them, his cousin was examining his room. "What do you want, Samira?"

"To help you."

"I don't need help. I'm fine."

"Okay, then I want to help with the graffiti," she said. "I want in."

Kareem looked up at Samira, startled, then back down at his sketchbook.

"I know it's hard being here," she said quietly. "I'm starting to get that more."

Kareem's throat tightened. He hated being constantly on the verge of tears.

"I'm really sorry," Samira continued. "I haven't been a good cousin." She took a deep breath, then exhaled. "I get why you were upset on your first day of school. I know I should have said something to Dylan. But it's hard to deal with that stuff all the time. I guess I've gotten used to ignoring it all. I just don't always know what to do." She paused again, as if to refocus her thoughts. When she next spoke, her voice cracked slightly. "But, Kareem, please talk to me. You're not okay."

He didn't know what to say. His eyes flooded with tears, and this time they overflowed, pouring down his face. Deep down, he knew he needed help. He *wasn't* okay. He was drowning. But he didn't know how his cousin could help.

He didn't want to tell her about Hassan and the picture and how he fell asleep every night worrying. Or that he felt useless here, thousands of miles from everything. Or the fact that he barely spoke to his parents. It was too much. If he let it all out, it would never go back in. He might not be able to get back up. Kareem wanted so much to control something, to feel like he mattered, to make sure his friends and parents would be safe. But he couldn't do any of those things.

Sam extended her hand to him. "Will you show me your other pieces?"

He handed her his sketchbook.

She flipped through the pages slowly. "I love this one." She pointed to the bird with no wings, on the tree with no roots.

Kareem's heart ached looking at it. How could he explain the bird with clipped wings was him?

"So what's our next piece?" asked Sam, looking serious.

"I don't know, Sam. I'm not in the mood."

"No, Kareem, you have to keep going." She patted the sketchbook, turned a few more pages, and stopped on the red mouth with thick lips and a silver tape gag. "This one was awesome!"

"Eleanora came up with it."

Sam's eyes widened.

Kareem thought about how different Eleanora's piece was to the picture Hassan had sent. Here, it was just play. People over there were gambling with their lives.

"Samira, what does it matter? People here don't care."

"That's why we have to do it! It's easy to avoid thinking about big world stuff when things around you are good. Or maybe . . . it's hard to think about things that you can't fix?" She shrugged. "I don't know. But this is important."

Kareem climbed onto his bed and grabbed a pillow. "I miss thinking about unimportant things, Samira." He leaned back. "Just a few months ago, all I cared about was soccer and friends and what was for dinner. How did I even get here?"

He rolled onto his side, hugging the pillow, and stared at the headboard. He closed his eyes, suddenly *so* tired.

"I wish I could help, Kareem." Samira put a hand on his back. "Insha'Allah everybody will be okay."

But she couldn't guarantee anything. Nobody could.

"And people *are* listening to you guys," she said. "They're sharing your stuff. It's like the most popular thing at school now."

Kareem hugged his pillow tighter. "What's the point, Samira? In Syria, it means something. We're asking for our freedom."

Sam placed the sketchbook in front of him.

"We can come up with something to show people what's happening over there. We can't join the revolution in Syria, but maybe we can get people in Allansdale to care more?" She grabbed some paper from the printer, settled next to him on the bed, and started sketching words in different styles.

Kareem nodded, only half-listening to her. He was still thinking about Hassan and Yusuf and the rest of the gang.

CHAPTER 25

SAMIRA

Sam finished the Spirit Squad's banner exactly to Cat's instructions. She loved the lion she'd drawn, but the letters were all wrong. Cat had insisted she make them big and put them smack dab in the banner's center. Sam leaned back in her chair and waited for the paint to dry. Across the art room, Amari was hunched over the soccer team's banner, perfecting a shattered glass look around a ball that was exploding out of the sign. She smiled.

He really is talented. Who would've known?

She turned her attention to her sketchbook, and the piece she wanted to do with Kareem, toying with a few ideas. She drew the Syrian flag with the word "freedom" in both Arabic and English, then tried: "We Want Freedom. Free Syria!" Would anyone in Allansdale even recognize the Syrian flag?

She drew a pot of boiling liquid and wrote "Freedom Is Bubbling." She smiled. That worked. She doodled some bubbles spewing out, and an idea clicked into place. On a clean page, she started over, getting more excited. She drew the pot of liquid again, this time with red, black, and white bubbles. Then she added green sputtering stars. Together, it was all the elements of the Syrian flag, escaping the pot. Wanting to be free.

She suddenly thought of a famous cartoonist whose art her dad kept framed on his desk at home. In it, army generals were scooping medals into the bowls of hungry Syrians. Hers would be different. There would be no scooping, only hungry people standing near the pot holding empty bowls, longing for the bubbling liquid—for a piece of their country, their flag, their future. No, wait, the people should be children. The future. Sam flipped the page again.

We're Hungry for Freedom.

The words were urgent. She imagined the hunger as something primal that ate away at you, and the freedom as something that nourished the soul. Together, they were fierce. She'd wanted this piece to be the one that introduced Syria to Allansdale. She wondered what it would feel like to do something like this in Syria, in beautiful Arabic text—bold but flowing, the taller letters pointing up to the sky. The hunger in the edges and empty spaces between words.

Sam smiled. It was perfect. Hopefully, Kareem would agree.

"Are you kidding me!" Amari yelled from the next table.

Sam startled. "What's wrong?"

"Cat. Again." He held up his phone. "She won't quit!"

Sam went over to him, and Amari handed her his phone. Cat had posted the most recent graffiti and placed red Xs over it. #Vandalism, #ArrestTheVandals, and #KeepOurStreetsClean.

"She's posting four or five a day," Amari said. "Everywhere! I can't believe so many people are resharing them! Plus, like, 'Arrest the Vandals, Keep Our Streets Clean?' She sounds like some grandma! Why does she care so much about graffiti? What's it to her?" He moved closer to her and scrolled down the screen. "Look at this one. She *really* wants the graffiti artist to get in trouble."

At that moment, the art room door swung open, and Cat, Avery, Lucy, and Dylan entered.

"Here comes Grandma Cop," muttered Amari. He raised his voice and said, "What's your problem, Cat? Why are you being such a hater?"

"What's *your* problem, Amari? Why are you so into vandalism?"

"Give me a break, Cat!" Amari looked at Sam in disbelief. "Vandalism is when you just destroy stuff. This is . . . it's . . . it's totally different."

"Yeah, it's *art*," mumbled Sam. "Art that says something."

"Have you even taken a second to think about what the graffiti is saying, Cat?" Amari moved to stand directly in front of her. "Did you actually *read* any of it?"

"Of course. But you can't just go around drawing on the library and city hall. It's not okay!" Cat looked at Avery and

Lucy for confirmation. "This is how it all starts. A little 'graffiti' and soon our town will be covered in ugly red paint, and we've turned into the ghetto. My parents donated money to build those places. I mean, they're, like, almost ours. People aren't allowed to just draw all over them."

"Argh, Cat, read the messages!" said Amari. "Wake up! Look outside your world, Cat Spencer! It's not even real paint! Most of the pieces are already gone!"

"I don't need this tantrum right now." Cat rolled her eyes. "I just came here to check out our banner." Cat glanced at the banner Sam had been working on and then turned around to leave, throwing her bag over her shoulder. "My dad said he's going to get to the bottom of it. He's making sure the cameras in all the public spaces are working, and he's requested that the city council install more, especially around the school after that sticker stunt. They know someone here is causing the trouble, and they're going to catch them." She looked right at Sam. "Oh, and he talked to the superintendent of schools yesterday. Any Allansdale student found responsible will be expelled."

The word "expelled" echoed over and over in Sam's head.

"Is that true, Dylan?" Amari asked. Dylan hadn't said a word since they came in. He shifted from side to side.

"Yeah, that's what Dad said at dinner."

Amari looked curiously at his best friend. "What about you? What's your take on all this?"

"I mean." Dylan shuffled his feet, looking awkward in a way Sam had never seen before. "I mean, the graffiti is totally cool. It's awesome. But . . . I also see what my dad's saying. You know, whoever it is, they can't do this all around town. It would get, like, messy."

"Wow." Sam suddenly felt sick. "Right. Because chalk is so . . ." She could barely look at Dylan. "It's so *messy*. No one could possibly erase it. With water!"

Dylan stared at her, shocked. She suddenly realized her sketchbook was wide open, and Cat was uncomfortably close.

"Sam, let's get out of here," said Amari.

"Yeah," said Sam. "This is so stupid!" She swooped over to the table, slammed her sketchbook shut, and grabbed her stuff.

Cat caught her arm as she passed. "I know Ellie has something to do with this, Sam. Who else is good at art and hates Spirit Squad this much? I mean, I've asked around, and the stickers were only in *our* school. There were, like, a million of them in the art room. I know it's her, and I'm going to prove it. And if you're helping or covering for her, I'll prove that, too."

Sam felt herself flush. She looked over at Lucy, who was biting her nails. Avery avoided eye contact. Sam tucked her chin into her chest so they couldn't read what was written on her face, then stomped out of the room. Amari followed as she broke into a run.

"Sam, slow down. Where are you going?" Amari caught up and gently grabbed her arm. "Man, you're fast."

Sam's face burned red. Maroon, maybe. Even darker. Cat really got her blood boiling. "Cat is just so . . . so . . . she's so . . . ARGH! I can't believe she's accusing Ellie just because she doesn't like her! She'd love it if Ellie got expelled. And what's with Dylan? Graffiti is *messy*? Give me a break." Sam looked at Amari's hand on her arm and felt the deep red drain from her face. Shoot, now she was all blush.

"I'll talk to him. He just doesn't get it yet. And, Cat—I don't know. Maybe when Dylan eventually gets it, he'll explain it to her."

Sam looked into Amari's dark brown eyes and nodded. "I just wish they weren't so . . . so . . ."

"Don't let them get to you, Sam." Amari nudged her as they headed for the exit. "You got to stay cool. Like me." Amari pointed to himself, closed his eyes, and lifted his chin in the air, before doing a full turn and smiling big.

"Right," said Sam, laughing.

"Plus, I got your back. We'll win this social media war because—" He paused and turned unusually serious. "Because we're right, Sam. Whoever is doing this is for real, and I don't know about you—but I'm in."

Sam nodded, warmth washing over her. "I have to go, Amari." She paused at the exit. "Thank you. You know, for having my back."

"At your service." Amari stood in the middle of the hallway and bowed.

"Oh my God, you're such a dork, Amari."

Sam bolted out of the school. Moments ago, she'd been furious, and now she was laughing. And smiling. And feeling all fuzzy inside. He was so ridiculous. And funny. And sweet.

She shook herself out of her daze. This was no time to think about Amari. She needed to warn Ellie and Kareem. She wasn't going to let her best friend and her cousin get expelled. Kareem couldn't afford to get in trouble for graffitiing *again*, not in Allansdale of all places. That's why his parents had sent him away in the first place.

Sam was panting by the time she arrived home. "Ellie, Kareem! Are you guys here?"

Nobody answered. She checked the living room and the kitchen, then ran downstairs. Nobody was home. She dashed across the street and banged on Ellie's door.

"Open up, Ellie, Kareem! Open up."

CHAPTER 26

KAREEM

Kareem and Ellie bent over a large drawing of a recycling sign, with blocky, upright letters that read REDUCE-REUSE-RECYCLE circling around it.

"What do you think?" asked Ellie. "I know it's simple. We could do more graffiti stickers. Or I was thinking, we could take a page out of the Spirit Squad handbook and do a banner this time. Maybe place it outside of the school?"

Kareem had been trying to figure out how to convince Hassan not to go ahead with his plan, when Ellie had shown up and begged Kareem to come over. Now, he shook his head. She had interrupted him for *this*? This was an ad campaign, *not* something worthy of graffiti. And worse, she was talking about stickers *again*. And banners?

"Why don't we just tell them who we are, Eleanora? We don't need graffiti for this. This is just . . ." He paused to make eye contact. "It's a school poster. I saw one the other day in the library. It even had the same symbol."

"It's not bad to remind people to recycle," said Ellie, putting her hands on her hips. "It's a different kind of revolution, to get people to care about what's happening to our Earth, Kareem. And, FYI, our school doesn't recycle. So it's a message they need to hear."

Kareem tensed. "I'm talking about freedom and a revolution, and you want to tell people to recycle? With stickers? And a banner? Sounds like a . . ." He took a deep breath. "A kindergarten project."

Kareem knew what Eleanora wanted to do was perfectly suitable for Allansdale. In fact, it was probably the right thing. But he couldn't help feeling disappointed. His parents and friends were dodging bullets. Recycling campaigns didn't seem like enough right now.

They heard banging on the door, and Sam's voice. "Open up, Ellie, Kareem! Open up!"

"Sam?" Ellie ran to open the front door. Kareem followed right behind her. Sam was outside, bent over, breathing hard.

"What's wrong?" said Ellie. "Are you okay?"

"Yeah, umm, give me a . . . sec." Sam came inside, trying to catch her breath. "Ya, I just ran . . . all the way . . . from school. Turns out . . . I'm a . . . little"—she gasped for air—"out of . . . shape." She dropped her bag on the floor but kept hold of her sketchbook. She led them into the living room and flopped onto the couch. "It's Cat Spencer. I mean, it's about the graffiti. I was at school . . . in the art room . . . and Cat came in."

"Samira, calm down." Kareem sat beside her. "Just breathe."

Beads of sweat ran down Samira's face. She breathed.

"Okay, shoo sar?" asked Kareem. "Explain."

Samira told him what had happened in the art room. "You could really get in trouble," she said finally. "Like, expelled trouble." She looked at them, wide-eyed. "Or maybe even arrested."

"Arrested? Are you serious!" yelled Ellie. "It's just chalk! I mean, most of it is already gone."

"I know, but they don't care. And Cat's especially on to you, Ellie."

"Me?" Ellie nearly choked. She cleared her throat. "Why— why ME?"

"I mean, because of the stickers, they're pretty sure it's a student at our school. And Cat's sure it's you because you hate Spirit Squad and because you're so good at art."

Kareem watched Eleanora and Samira as they went back and forth talking about Cat Spencer, arrests and expulsions, and the Spencer family. For the first time since he'd arrived in Allansdale, he was witnessing their friendship up close.

Samira was clearly worried about Ellie. And Ellie looked worried, too. Kareem knew Ellie masked her anxiety with humor—it was exactly what Hassan did. But she wasn't even throwing out one-liners. She was just sitting on the couch, her knee nervously shaking.

"The Spencers are turning this into a full-on campaign, Sam," wailed Ellie, looking to Kareem. "And Cat's focused on me!"

Kareem tried not to roll his eyes. He scooted over to the drawing, grabbed a pencil that was lying on the ground, and pretended to examine the poster again. Why were they taking this girl so seriously? They were treating Cat like she ran the town. To him, she was a spoiled, entitled bully. Period. He knew kids just like her in Syria, kids whose parents were important people. Everybody knew they had "connections," so they stayed away from them. For some reason, he hadn't thought that sort of thing happened in the United States. He wasn't sure why. Maybe because his uncle said things worked differently here. But apparently, some things were the same everywhere.

Did they seriously think they'd be put in jail for some chalk? Who cares if the city council adds more cameras? We'll just take more precautions.

"Maybe we should hold off until things calm down," said Sam. "Just for a few days. Or maybe a couple of weeks?"

Kareem looked at the girls incredulously. "Are you kidding? Someone's a little upset because a brat is complaining about chalk on buildings, and you're just going to stop?" He laughed and put down the pencil. "This is what I mean about being here. It's just . . . it's just . . . I don't know. It's like people don't *really* care about anything. Rules are more important than what's happening in the world."

He looked at the rolled-out paper on the floor. "I have to go." He got up, grabbed his backpack, and headed for the door.

"Kareem, wait a second." Ellie stood and reached for his shoulder. "Can we talk about this? It's okay to take a break and . . . assess."

Kareem freed himself. "No, I have to go. I'll see you later."

He left her and Sam standing in the foyer and walked to the park. Hassan hadn't texted him back yet. He searched for Spray Man, and admired his last piece, DOWN WITH THE TRAITOR. He had been getting bolder in recent weeks.

An alert sounded for breaking news on #SyriaNews: "Spray Man Arrested."

Kareem's heart stopped. They'd caught him. Ramy! Was it Ramy? What if they had Hassan, too? Is that why he hadn't answered?

Kareem sat under a tree in the park, clutching his sketchbook. Sam and Ellie were worried about getting expelled, while Spray Man was in a Syrian prison. Kareem prayed again. He prayed that Ramy was okay. He wasn't positive that Ramy *was* Spray Man. But he couldn't shake the hunch. He texted Yusuf and waited. Five minutes. Ten. Fifteen. He sat and stared at his phone, his heart pounding in his chest, his hands sweaty. No answer came. Maybe Yusuf had been arrested, too.

He wanted to throw up, but instead he laid his head on his backpack and tucked his legs into his chest. Thinking about his friends and his parents brought tears to his eyes again. He choked them back until they disappeared. Then he checked his watch.

It was the middle of the night in Damascus.

They're all sleeping. Calm down, Kareem. Calm down.

He was exhausted, and for the first time in weeks, completely and utterly alone. There was nobody around him. Nobody who understood him. Not even Eleanora.

He sat up and started to scribble, the empty space inside him filling with anger. This place was so perfect, so prim and proper.

"Wake up, everybody! LOOK AROUND YOUR WORLD!" he screamed into the night air, at the top of his lungs. "Fee'ou! Iftahou 'Ayounkon!"

Nobody heard him but the chirping crickets. They didn't really care. Kareem sat on the manicured lawn of the park and stared into the sky. What did the sky above Damascus look like right now? He wondered how his parents were doing. He thought about Spray Man and Hassan and Yusuf and George. Where were they? He prayed they were okay and turned back to his sketchbook. He ripped out his last attempt and crumpled it up.

He had no idea what to draw.

CHAPTER 27

SAMIRA

Sam and Ellie stood in the foyer of Ellie's house, stunned.

"Sam, he's so angry."

"I know. We have to go talk to him." Sam picked up her jacket and headed for the door, but Ellie grabbed her arm.

"I think he needs a little space, Sam."

Sam paused. Of course people needed space sometimes. But she'd given him *too much* space before. What was the right amount of space to give someone? She followed Ellie back into the living room. They hadn't been alone together for weeks. Ellie sat back down in front of the rolled-out paper in the living room, and Sam joined her.

"I mean, we probably wouldn't get arrested," Ellie said. "I've never heard of kids going to jail for using chalk on sidewalks. That's basically what we're doing. Drawing with chalk. Just . . . on walls."

Sam rubbed the back of her neck. "Yeah, I'm more worried about getting expelled."

Ellie looked so upset. Sam had a sudden urge to hug her, to tell her she missed her, to say she was sorry. She'd missed sitting next to her best friend.

They both spoke at once.

"Ellie—"

"Sam—"

"You go first," said Ellie.

"I, uh, wanted to say . . ." She knew what she wanted to say. That she had been wrong. That Cat was a jerk. That Ellie had been right. But the words got stuck in her throat. Why couldn't she say them? Panicked, she instead tackled Ellie with a big hug.

They giggled when Sam finally let go.

"I've missed you, Eleanora Gold," said Sam. "I'm sorry."

"Me too. I'm sorry, too."

Sam breathed a sigh of relief. Ellie was back. In that moment, she felt the universe realign.

"I wasn't a very good friend," said Ellie. "I don't like Cat. And I still think she was using you. But that's why I *should* have gone with you to that meeting. *Because* I don't trust her. And I should have helped you with the banner. I'm sorry, Sam. I was harsh."

Sam smiled. "Thanks. But you were right about her. I should have listened to you. I know you were just watching out for me. I really do like Lucy, though. She's sweet. And . . . and so is Amari."

"Amari?" said Ellie, in a teasing voice. "Amari, sweet? Okay, I see. Amari I approve of. You have my blessings."

202

"Blessings?" said Sam, laughing. "You're ridiculous. But I never want us to stop talking again. That was terrible."

Ellie stuck out her pinkie. "Me neither. Let's say, no no talking for more than twenty-four hours tops. Ever. I mean, if we're in a fight. Not because we went on vacation or something and couldn't call."

Sam laughed. They squeezed pinkies and hugged each other again.

"Okay, back to Kareem," said Ellie. "And this whole mess."

Sam opened her sketchbook to show Ellie.

"I drew this at school today. We could simplify it. I'm going to send it to Kareem."

Ellie admired the sketch of the boiling pot of liquid as Sam thought about Kareem and how he had stormed out of the house.

"Ellie, they're arresting and shooting at protesters now," said Sam. "We have to help him. He could do something . . . I don't know . . . something stupid."

"What could he do? He can't really get on a plane back to Syria. And what can we do? We can't keep graffitiing if they're on to us." Ellie lowered her eyes. "Or, if they're on to me. I mean, we already ditched the cop in the park. We might be pushing it."

"Yeah," Sam agreed, "you need to lie low for a while. I'll do the next piece with Kareem. We should get you an alibi, so people know it wasn't you."

Ellie nodded, but her eyes were wide with concern.

"I'm going to try to talk to him," said Sam, a knot forming in her stomach.

Ever since fourth grade, she had kept her head down at school and stayed out of Cat Spencer's way. And all she had wanted, so desperately, was to be a part of Spirit Squad, to no longer feel excluded, to draw and work on banners with a bunch of friends.

Now, she wanted more. She wanted her aunt and uncle to be safe. She wanted to support the protesters. But what could she, a Syrian American girl from Allansdale, do about a revolution taking place half a world away? For a second, she wondered how it would feel to be part of something so big and important. She wished banners carried more power. She wished they carried messages that could change the world around her—not only at her school, but in her whole town, and maybe even . . .

Sam jumped up, her eyes suddenly bright.

"I got it! I know something else you can work on now, too. What if we used the banner competition to raise awareness? Like for Syria? I mean, it's still small. It won't change what's happening there, but . . ."

Ellie lit up. "I love that idea! We could get the word out at school about what's happening in Syria, without getting expelled."

"And then we could also do a fundraiser." Sam took out her phone. "Maybe we can surprise Kareem with it? I have to text Amari about this."

"Right, we definitely need to text Amari," said Ellie, grinning. "Sam and Amari, sitting in a tree . . ."

"Ellie! Are you in kindergarten?"

"Sorry, I mean . . . Sam and Amari painting a banner. P-A-I-N-T-I-N-G."

Sam laughed and shook her head, texting rapidly.

Sam

> We need to talk. Have an idea for a new banner we can do together. Meet at lunch?

Amari

> I'll be there.

Sam smiled. He'd surprised her so many times in the last few weeks. Unlike Dylan, Amari had surprised her in a good way. His banner was so cool—she had no idea he was so talented. He even knew who Seen UA and Banksy were. And he'd totally had her back with Cat and Dylan.

She flipped back to the sketch. It was time to go all in—to take on Cat Spencer, and to make her mark on their school, Spirit Squad, and her cousin. She had to stop hiding. Amari wasn't afraid, so why should she be? She sent Kareem a message.

CHAPTER 28

KAREEM

Kareem's phone vibrated as he lay on the grass, looking up at the sky. His heart leaped, hoping Hassan had finally replied, but it was only Samira.

She'd sent a hand-drawn picture of a vibrantly colored pot with stripes, bubbles, and stars in white, black, red, and green. Beside it, kids were holding empty bowls. Above, the words "We Need Freedom" in Arabic. Kareem smiled. It looked like a riff on a cartoon by the famous Syrian cartoonist Ali Ferzat. Sam must have seen it somewhere.

Maybe he'd underestimated his cousin. Maybe she understood more than he gave her credit for. He liked the idea of kids holding empty bowls. And the bubbles were the colors of the Syrian flag. The picture seemed to convey the hope that, one day, they could have a piece of their own country.

He wished he could send it to Ramy or Hassan. He texted Hassan again and then got up and brushed the grass off his slightly damp pants. Maybe Hassan would respond this time.

It had been more than twenty-four hours, and Kareem hadn't been able to reach *any* of his friends.

He headed back to his aunt and uncle's house. He was still angry, but he no longer wanted to punch a hole in a wall. How could he work with people who were afraid of spraying chalk on walls? How could he explain that if they wanted change, they had to take risks? Deep down, he knew it wasn't Samira and Eleanora's fault. Before the revolution, he would have cared about getting in trouble as well.

He stopped at the front door of his aunt and uncle's home and closed his eyes. He imagined that he was about to walk into his own apartment, in Syria. Maybe his mom would have made his favorite foods, lahmeh bil ajeen or sheikh mahshe. Or her favorite, mujaddara. Or his dad's, koussa mahshe. He had smelled them in Allansdale, too, but it wasn't only the food he missed. It was the doorman, Abou Abdo, who would play soccer with Kareem on random afternoons. It was the falafel place a few doors down, the sound of cars outside, the random voices of their neighbors.

He opened the door and heard only the chatter of the television. Samira was on the couch, with the remote control in her hand.

"Thank you for the picture," Kareem said, pausing at the top of the stairwell. "I'm going to my room."

Samira bolted from the couch and placed her body between Kareem and the stairs. "Not so fast, Mr. Graffiti."

"I'm not in the mood for this, Samira," he said. "Can you please move?"

"No." She looked him firmly in the eyes. "I need to talk to you."

Kareem stepped back and folded his arms. "Okay, then talk."

Samira dragged him over to the couch and sat next to him.

"Kareem, I want to do a piece with you here in Allansdale," said Samira, her eyes wide with excitement. "I want to help."

"Wait a minute," said Kareem. "What happened? A couple hours ago, you and Eleanora were afraid of getting arrested. And now you are in? I'm confused."

Sam pulled out her notebook. "Well, since Cat's on to Ellie, we decided she's going to take a little break. When we do the next piece, we'll make sure she has an alibi."

Kareem rolled his eyes a little, and Sam said, "Come on, Kareem. She really wants to help. And I . . . I want to help. I should have been helping all this time."

Kareem stared at the television. He knew Samira was being sincere, but she didn't really seem like the graffiti type. She made banners, and joined groups like Spirit Squad.

"Samira, you just don't get it," he said, hunching his shoulders.

Sam nodded and quietly said, "Okay. Maybe you can explain it to me."

Kareem looked up at the ceiling, then back at his cousin. Her eyes were big and earnest. He wanted to help her understand, he just wasn't sure exactly how to explain it all. "You know, a few months ago, my life wasn't much different than yours. I was in my home, I had my family around me and best friends. I played soccer. There was even a girl in my class, she was so pretty and . . . umm . . ." He paused, blushed, and glanced back at the ceiling. "Never mind. Anyhow, when the revolution started, things changed."

He told Samira the entire story—about the kids from Dara'a and Hamza; the protests; the talks with Ramy; the graffiti; the shabiha; and how his parents had sent him away, against his will. He told her about Hassan's text, and how worried he was that Hassan or Yusuf or Ramy or George would get caught—or might already have been caught. He had never said it all out loud. He closed his eyes while he talked to keep the tears from coming. He couldn't believe this was his life.

Samira listened in silence.

"We weren't asking for permission, Samira. Freedom, by its definition, does not require permission. We are demanding our freedom." He paused. "A graffiti artist named Spray Man tagged that phrase all over Damascus a few weeks ago." He swallowed hard, struggling to force the next sentence out. "A few days ago, he was arrested. I think Spray Man is my friend Ramy. And when you're arrested in Syria, sometimes you're never heard from again. They're called 'the disappeared.' And we have thousands of disappeared in Syria. There are moms who have no idea what happened to their children—and for years, they ask questions, they hope. It's one thing to lose someone you love. It's an entirely other thing to have no idea—for months or years—if the person you love is even alive or dead. What's happening here in Allansdale, it's just play. We're talking about spraying simple messages in chalk, and if we can't even stand by that, I don't know what to say."

After a long pause, Samira said: "I get it. I understand."

"So? Are you ready? What if you get in trouble? Are you ready for Cat?"

Sam tapped on her sketchbook and looked right at Kareem. "I'm ready. And I have ideas. What did you think of what I sent you? You never told me."

"It's really good, Samira," he said with a big smile.

She broke into a huge, relieved grin, her whole face lighting up.

They went downstairs and Kareem spread his large pad of paper out on the living room floor. They talked about Cat's hashtag war and how her latest—#GraffitiIsVandalism #ArrestTheVandals—had more than five hundred shares between them in just the last few hours.

"Why is she so obsessed with this?" asked Kareem.

"I don't know." Sam tapped her pen on the paper. "Hey, I love the idea you just mentioned. 'Freedom Does Not Require Permission.' Maybe we can do something like that?"

Kareem nodded. "Yeah, it's good, huh? But maybe we need to reply directly to Cat's posts about the graffiti."

Sam jumped up. "How about 'Get with the Spirit. Freedom Requires No Permission.'"

Kareem looked at Samira, surprised. He hadn't expected her to be this good, this quickly. She stared at what she had written, frantically twisting a curl near her ear. She was nervous, but he was proud of her.

"Is that what we really want to say, though?" asked Kareem, slowing them down. "Our point is that graffiti isn't vandalism, it's freedom of speech. *And* we want to say that freedom doesn't wait for permission. So what we really want to say is that graffiti does not require permission."

"That's it, Kareem. That's it!" Samira jumped up and down in excitement. "You just said it. 'Graffiti Requires No Permission. Get with the Spirit.' It's a direct response to Cat, but it also says exactly what we want."

Kareem smiled. "You're good at this."

Sam blushed. "Thanks." She nodded and mulled it over. "You know, I don't think this one needs a picture. It's all letters. It's definitely a bold cursive, and the two f's would be perfectly symmetrical. The G large and bold . . ."

Kareem listened to her explain each letter: how the A was radical and crisp, how the I's would be topped with a large, strong dot. Suddenly, Sam sat back down on the floor.

"Wait, I've got it, Kareem. This is even better."

She wrote something in an arithmetic-styled font. Kareem peered over her shoulder and grinned—it was perfect! Her letters said it all:

GRAFFITI = ART + ACTIVISM = ARTIVISM

GET WITH THE SPIRIT

CHAPTER 29

SAMIRA

Sam held the spray chalk can upright, her hands shaking.

"Is this crooked?" she asked, turning around to look for Kareem, who was surveying the main road.

"It's fine, Samira," whispered Kareem. "Yalla, keep going."

Sam sprayed every letter as big as she could, gaining confidence as she went. She wasn't used to working on such a big, upright canvas. Her heart pounded so hard she was sure her letters looked like they belonged in an ad for a horror movie. But when she stepped back to look, the letters were smooth and proud. Slightly tilted, but not bad for a first-timer.

GRAFFITI = ART + ACTIVISM = ARTIVISM, all in an arithmetic-styled font, all in black.

GET WITH THE SPIRIT in a bold red cursive, right below it.

"Let's go, Samira, out," said Kareem, pulling her arm.

"Wait, a picture!" Samira said.

They took a selfie, packed up, and walked swiftly toward the park.

Sam bounced on her toes, unable to contain herself, the empty spray chalk cans clanking around in her backpack. Sam's mind, her limbs, her fingers, every inch of her body tingled. They had sneaked out of the house at five a.m. and rushed straight to the Red Cross building, right next to their school. She felt like the star of her own action-packed spy movie, with her own soundtrack playing in her head.

They hung around the park for an hour and then headed to school in time for breakfast in the cafeteria.

"I still can't believe we did that. I mean, I did that! Look at my hands—they're still shaking!" Samira said, her hand raised in midair. "That was so . . . so . . . awesome. Did I say awesome?"

"Yes, you did," said Kareem, laughing. "You need to work on your face—what do they call it? When you hide your feelings?"

"Oh yeah, I have no poker face," Sam said, bouncing in her seat. "So, what's next? Should we do something tomorrow?"

"Calm down, little one," said Kareem, with a smile.

Sam's phone vibrated with new Twitter alerts. "Oh my god, Kareem, it's happening," she burst out. "They're sharing it!"

"Samira, remember, poker face," Kareem said. "Tawley balik."

"Okay, okay, I'm cool!" she yelled. She dropped her voice and whispered, "That was a little loud. Sorry. And I am being patient."

He laughed. "Meet you outside after school," he said in Arabic.

Sam abandoned her tray and skipped toward the stairwell. She couldn't wait to see Ellie's reaction. At her locker, she opened her backpack carefully so that nobody could see the cans inside. She grabbed her math textbook, closed her locker, and turned to find Cat Spencer standing right next to her.

"Hi, Sam," she said, with a big fake smile. "Want to sign our petition? Say no to vandalism."

"Nah, I'm good, thanks." She said it as calmly as she could. Which was not very.

"Seriously, you're not going to sign?" Cat's eyes narrowed. Her arms folded around her clipboard. "Are you trying to protect Ellie?"

Ignore her. Walk away.

"So it *is* Ellie. Silence is basically admitting it's true," Cat said, her voice rising. "I knew it."

Sam glanced over her shoulder to check if anyone was listening, then she hissed, "Cat, why on earth would Ellie do this? And even if she did, so what? It's just chalk. My question is, why would you accuse someone without proof?"

"Let's just say it's a hunch," said Cat. "Come to think of it, maybe your cousin's part of it, too? He's sort of quiet, and they're always together. And graffiti wasn't a problem before he got here."

Sam felt her face turn bright red. She wanted to scream at Cat, to tell her to get a life, mind her own business, and grow up. But all she could do was turn around and walk away.

"Or maybe it's you, Sam Sukkari," Cat yelled down the hallway after her. "Maybe you're behind this. I mean, why else would you be so upset? And like my dad always says, Muslims are behind all kinds of problems these days."

The hairs on Sam's neck stood up. She could hear her heart pounding in her ears.

She doesn't matter, she doesn't matter, she doesn't matter, she doesn't matter.

Sam repeated it over and over to herself as she continued walking. Why couldn't she ever find the words when she needed them?

You're a bully, Cat Spencer. You're a spoiled, entitled, mean bully. You only know how to put people down. You have no idea what graffiti is.

Any of those would have been fine. They would have been better than the barely audible mumbling and blank stare she'd actually given. Even a simple "get a life, Cat Spencer." But she had said nothing. She needed to say something, anything. She owed it to Ellie and Kareem. And to herself.

She was thinking about exactly what she would say to Cat next time, when the image of Amari standing up to Cat came back to her. She took out her phone and texted him.

Sam

UGH. CAT SPENCER IS SUCH A JERK!

216

She felt better after texting him. He would totally understand. It was easy to talk to him, and he always had her back. She smiled thinking about how he'd saluted her in the hallway when she'd called him Mr. Modest, how he'd gently touched her arm to calm her down. And then it hit her. She didn't like him a little bit. She had a huge *I'm thinking about him with a goofy smile on my face* crush on Amari. She was *so* over Dylan Spencer. How could she have ever liked him? They had so little in common, and he didn't even think for himself. Half the time he followed Amari's lead, the other half he parroted his dad. He just didn't get it. At all.

"Samira Sukkari." Ellie ran up to her from behind and gave her a big hug. She lowered her voice. "It's awesome!"

What's awesome?" said Sam, confused.

"Helloooo, Samira Sukkari!" said Ellie, as she grabbed her and looked into her eyes.

"Your piece! Wake up!"

The run-in with Cat had almost made Sam forget what she'd accomplished just a few hours ago.

"Okay, what's happening here?" Ellie's eyes narrowed suspiciously. "Your face is red and you're just standing still, all by yourself in a hallway." She broke into a knowing smile. "I know what's wrong with you! Or at least I can guess." Her smile grew. "Where is he?"

"Ellie! Stop! I'm actually really upset right now." Sam turned around, trying to hide her own smile.

How are you even smiling, Samira Sukkari? After what just happened with Cat?

"You don't look upset," Ellie said. "You look embarrassed. You know, the I-like-someone kind of embarrassed."

"Fine, don't believe me," Sam retorted.

"Samira, Ellie, what are you two still doing here?" Mrs. Jones, the English teacher, said from behind them. "Let's move. The bell is about to ring!"

"Gotta go," said Sam, starting to walk away, but Ellie caught up and locked arms with her.

"I'm sorry, I'm sorry," Ellie said. "Of course I believe you. What happened?"

On the way to class, Sam told her what Cat had said. As they entered the classroom, Sam froze at the sight of Cat seated in the third row, eyeing them with her icy, dagger-like letters. Sam instinctively lowered her head, but Ellie gave her arm a squeeze and smiled. Ellie raised her eyebrows, Arab-style, and Sam smiled back. Ellie had learned to speak Arabic eyebrows before either of them could read. Then Ellie and Sam raised their heads and stalked past Cat to their seats. She might not have come up with a snappy comeback for Cat, but she had Ellie's confident, unwavering letters by her side.

CHAPTER 30

KAREEM

Kareem walked behind Sam and Ellie as they made their way home, listening to their conversation about Cat and her petition. He was glad they couldn't see him rolling his eyes. He had no idea why they all thought this rude girl was such a big deal.

"And I didn't even say anything," Samira said. "It was like my brain froze up."

Ellie put her arm around Samira. "Come on, you'll stand up to her next time. She just took you by surprise. Anyway, it's not like Cat Spencer is going to listen to anybody."

Kareem interrupted them. "Forget Cat. The best way to deal with her is through the graffiti itself."

Sam looked back at him. "But she's on to us. I mean, she's accused me *and* you *and* Ellie now. It feels like a matter of time before we get caught."

"So?" Kareem said. "And?"

"Kareem, I know you think this isn't important, but it sort of is. Her dad is a big shot in Allansdale. And did you hear what Cat said? Expelled!" Sam's voice rose. "Doesn't that matter, just a little?"

Kareem sighed. They'd been through this less than twenty-four hours ago, and now here they were again. Of course, he didn't want anyone to get expelled, but they had more important things to do than worry about Cat Spencer and her petition.

"Let's talk about our next piece," he said, trying to change the subject. He ignored the look they gave each other and started rattling off ideas, speaking loudly as if he could cut through their worry with volume. "Maybe it's time to do something about Syria directly. Something simple, like 'Help Syria.' Or we could do a 'Graffiti Is Freedom' piece. Or how about 'Enough Is Enough? It's Time to Care. #FreeSyria.'"

"If we make it about Syria, they'll definitely know it's us," said Ellie, frowning in confusion, as if he didn't realize this.

"We actually have another idea, Kareem," Sam jumped in. "We've been talking about doing a banner about Syria for the school competition. Amari's in on it, too. We weren't going to tell you because we wanted to surprise you."

Kareem walked in silence. They wanted to turn their city-wide graffiti campaign into a silly banner competition. He had already conceded to using chalk and stickers. He clenched his fists, ready to snap at them, but then caught a glimpse of Ellie's pale face. For a moment, he saw Hassan. It had been five days since Hassan's text, and in that moment, Kareem could only see his anxious brown eyes as he stood in front of the sandy-colored wall, yelling, "You know that's too risky!" Kareem had stayed up late every night trying to get more information about his friends. Hassan's various Twitter accounts were still silent. None of his other friends had texted back. When Ellie opened her mouth to speak, Kareem heard Hassan's voice asking him to slow down, to think about things, to do something more measured.

Kareem had been trying to distract himself with the graffiti, telling himself that everyone was okay, that it was only the time difference making it hard for them to connect. But he couldn't distract himself any longer. He was doing to Samira and Eleanora what he had done to Hassan. He was pushing them too far, way beyond their comfort zones. And now Hassan was probably in trouble because of him.

"Kareem, are you okay?" asked Ellie, snapping her fingers in front of his eyes. "What's happening?"

"You look like you've seen a ghost or something," said Sam.

Kareem realized they'd somehow reached home already. "I'm fine."

Samira took out her key. "Did you hear what we said about the banner competition idea?" She looked back at him as she opened the front door.

He followed her in, about to answer, but fell silent when he saw his uncle and aunt in the living room. What were they doing home in the middle of the day? They had been talking intensely but fell silent as their eyes landed on him. Kareem's heart stopped. *Mama? Baba? Hassan?*

"What's happening?" asked Kareem, his voice rising, panic clawing at his chest.

"Kareem, please come here, take a seat near me," his uncle said. "We need to talk to you."

"No." He began to shake, his mouth going dry. "No. What's happening? Are they okay? Why are you home so early? Are Mama and Baba okay? Is Hassan okay?"

"Your parents are okay, Kareem. Alhamdulillah," Khalo Ahmed said. "I don't know who Hassan is, but I'm sure he's fine, too." He paused for a moment, as though figuring out what to say. "Habibi, your parents' hospital was bombed this afternoon. They're completely fine. But we wanted you to know before you saw it on the news."

Kareem staggered over to the sofa and his knees buckled. He fell into the cushions, letting his backpack drop to the floor. "What? A *bomb*?"

The hospital he had visited so often while his parents finished their patient rounds; the hospital where he would draw as a child. *That* hospital had been *bombed*? Samira and Ellie stood in the entryway, their mouths agape. They looked like frozen statues, staring at him.

Khalo Ahmed looked at Kareem seriously. "Yes, but they are okay," he said again. "I just spoke with them."

"I want to talk to them, I need to talk to them!" Kareem's voice wobbled as it got louder. "I need to talk to my mom. I need to talk to her."

"Of course, habibi. We'll try them again. But if they don't answer, I don't want you to panic. They're dealing with an emergency, helping their patients. I need you to trust me that they're okay."

Kareem nodded. He tried to imagine what it would feel like to be in a building that had been bombed. Did the building shake? Did walls come crumbling down around them? How many people were hurt?

Amo picked up his phone and called. "Allo, Allo, ya Farah, Kareem bido yahkee ma'kon," he said to Kareem's mom. "He knows, but he needs to talk to you." He handed the phone to Kareem.

"Mama, Mama, are you okay?" Kareem said in Arabic, tears streaming down his face. "Are you okay? What happened?"

His mom sobbed on the other side of the line. "Habibi, alhamdulillah, we are okay. We were on the other side of the hospital. Everything shook, and the lights and windows all shattered. And . . ."

She fell quiet, though Kareem could still hear faint sobs coming from the other side. A few seconds later, his father picked up the phone.

"Habibi, we are fine," he said. "Just take care of yourself and your uncle and your cousin. I promise you, we are okay. We will not lie to you. Alhamdulillah, Allah sattar."

Kareem listened to his father's words and stopped crying. His voice shook. "Baba, you have to leave. You have to come here."

There was a pause on the line. "Not yet, habibi. We will talk about it later. We have to go; a lot of patients need us right now. I love you, Kareem." His dad's voice cracked in the middle of the word "bahi"—"bak": I love you. "*We* love you. Have faith, habibi. It will all be okay. Insha'Allah. Don't forget to pray."

The line went silent.

"Habibi, let's have dinner," said Tant Ranya, coming over to Kareem to give him a hug. Kareem let her wrap her arms around him, but his body was numb, his mind blank. Samira and Ellie still hadn't moved. He wanted to go to his room and never come up again.

He wriggled free of Tant Ranya's embrace. They were all looking at him anxiously. He knew they cared. His uncle must be as worried as he was about his mom. She was his sister, after all. But Kareem just couldn't do this anymore. He wasn't supposed to be here. He didn't want his uncle consoling him. He wanted to hug his mom and dad and know they were safe. He wanted his old life back.

"Can I please go to my room?" he asked, trying to hold back more tears. "I'm not hungry."

Khalo Ahmed nodded, and Kareem ran downstairs. He threw his backpack on the floor, jumped onto his bed, and hit his pillow as hard as he could. In an instant, his parents could have been gone forever. Poof. Just like that. He could have lost them both. He punched his pillow over and over again and then screamed into it. It didn't ease the ache in his chest.

He curled up and texted Hassan again.

Nothing.

Every time he thought he was getting a handle on something—on his feelings, on the graffiti, on his friends—it all unraveled again. And with each day that passed, things back home grew more and more uncertain. And, now, dangerous. First the protests, the arrests, and the gunfire into the crowds, and now a bomb. In his parents' hospital.

There was a knock at the door, but he didn't move.

"Kareem," Sam said from the other side of the door. "Baba sent me to check on you."

Kareem stayed silent. Another knock.

"Kareem, are you okay?" Sam said, softly.

Kareem wished he didn't have to answer. "Samira, I'm tired." He rolled over, so his back was to the door. "I'm going to take a nap. I'll come up a little later."

The door creaked as Samira slowly opened it. "I really think you should come upstairs and join us. I don't want to leave you alone like this."

Kareem didn't turn over. "Sam, please, just go away."

"Okay, just . . . we're here for you." After a pause, she added, "We love you." She gently closed the door behind her.

Kareem's eyes filled with tears as her footsteps faded. He didn't know why he kept pushing them away except that he couldn't handle all their sympathy on top of all his anger and resentment. But they wouldn't leave him alone for long. It wasn't the way Arab families did things. His uncle would probably come down next. So he grabbed his notebook and snuck out the basement door. He ran across the street to Ellie's treehouse and climbed up the ladder. It looked like it hadn't been used in years. A large limb grew through its center, and the cushions that lined the sides had browned from the weather. He sat down and opened his sketchbook.

Iman. Faith. It was the word his father had used. He knew his parents had it. What else would keep them in that hospital, helping patients, during such uncertain times, when an explosion had rocked the building? Kareem wanted to have faith. But how? How could he have faith that everything would be okay? That his parents would be safe? That Hassan and Yusuf and George and Ramy were all right? Other people had been arrested. Many had even been killed. How could he know that his parents and friends would be spared? And what about those poor people who hadn't been spared? What did that mean?

He drew a large building, with missiles raining down on it. He drew a boy watching from a nearby hill, showing no reaction. He added a bucket of popcorn next to him, as though he were in a movie theater. Above it, he wrote: "Syria Is BURN-ING and NOBODY CARES." This one had to be permanent. This one was real.

Kareem climbed down the treehouse ladder and ran back to his room. He checked his closet for the cans of spray paint that he and Ellie had bought on their first trip to the hardware store together. They'd planned to use them on paper.

He looked at the cans of real paint, his eyes fierce, hands sweaty. This was it. The time had come. He prepared a bag and set his alarm for three thirty a.m. He'd be expelled for sure. Without school, what would he do here? His uncle and aunt would *have* to send him home. The current arrangement wasn't working. They knew it. He knew it. This would be the most important piece yet. Not only would it tell the world what was really happening, it would get him sent home to his parents and friends. To his country. This piece would solve all his problems.

This one, he would do alone. And he would sign it.

Kareem Haddad. Spray Boy.

CHAPTER 31

SAMIRA

Sam tossed and turned. She had been trying to sleep for more than an hour, but she couldn't get the look on Kareem's face out of her head. That moment, when he'd thought something had happened to his parents, and then the conversation with his mom and dad, had been the scariest and saddest thing she'd ever witnessed. She had wanted to give him a hug, to tell him everything was going to be okay. But her aunt and uncle's hospital had just been bombed. *Bombed!*

She tried to imagine coming home to the same news about her parents but couldn't. For the first time, she appreciated that every night, she fell asleep in her own bed, with her parents sound asleep in the next room, and her best friends close by. She knew Kareem had been worried about Hassan for days. And now this.

She thought about going back downstairs to check on him again, but she stopped herself. He was probably sleeping. And while her mom might be right about not always giving people space, receiving "bombing news" definitely deserved some. She decided to check on him first thing in the morning. Instead, she started working on the Syria banner for the contest.

Samira tapped her pencil against her lips. What could they draw? The symbol of freedom? Doves? She thought about the pot. Maybe she could repurpose that one? Or do something with the clocks Kareem had described?

She thought of her aunt and uncle. They needed help. Maybe she could raise money for the hospital. She felt a rush of excitement as she thought about real ways they could help. Maybe they could do a bake sale. Or a walkathon for Syria. She wrote ideas on the side of the page. She sketched and wrote until she finally fell asleep with the sketchbook still in her lap around two a.m.

When she woke, it was already seven o'clock. She got dressed and ran straight down to Kareem's room. She knocked, but heard nothing.

"Kareem, I'm coming in, okay?" she warned as she pushed his door open. His bed was perfectly made, as if he hadn't slept in it. Kareem was gone. Where had he left so early? She tried calling him, but it went straight to voicemail. Sam exited the basement door and ran across the street. She texted Ellie.

Sam

Come out. Need to talk to you. Is Kareem with you?

Ellie appeared, her mouth full, looking confused. "Hey, Sam, what's up? Why didn't you just ring the doorbell?"

"Is Kareem here?" Sam asked. "He's not at home."

"No, he's not here." Ellie's eyes widened. "Let me get my backpack."

A few minutes later, she stumbled out of her house. They walked to school, debating where they should look first. Maybe the park? Was he out graffitiing again? They discussed the other possible graffiti sites that he had mentioned.

"Uh, why are the principal and teachers and band members standing outside of school?" Ellie said as they got closer. "What's happening?"

They were all looking up at the front of the school.

"OH . . . MY . . . GOD," said Sam, taking it all in. "He did it."

They joined the crowd staring at the freshly painted wall, speechless. A building in flames, with missiles and raindrops coming down all around. Next to it, spread across a little mound, sat a group of stick figures watching the show.

SYRIA IS BURNING AND NOBODY CARES was written in large, blocky, bright red letters. Then, at the bottom, the tagline KAREEM HADDAD, SPRAY BOY.

"He signed it!" Sam looked at Ellie, her mouth agape.

"I see that," said Ellie slowly. "Umm, I . . . I . . . I . . . guess we don't have to do that banner anymore. I think this gets the message across."

"Why would he do this? What was he thinking?"

The word "burning" was a fierce crimson, the edges jagged. The other letters were thick and rushed and urgent. Together, they were screaming. Desperate. Calling for help. Sam's chest tightened. It was all so painful.

Then it hit her. "Oh my God, Ellie. He's trying to get himself expelled. He wants to get sent home." She paused and thought a bit more. "Except that's not going to happen. They won't send him home when things are getting worse. Especially not after this."

Students slowly trickled in, and more than a few snapped photos. Teachers yelled at them to put their phones away and go inside.

Sam took out her own phone. "We have to fix this before it gets out of hand." She opened Twitter and the school boards, and her stomach lurched. "Or . . . maybe it's already out of hand. Cat's sharing it everywhere, Ellie. Look at this!"

She angled the screen to show Ellie the new hashtags: #ExpelKareemNow and #HaddadMustGo.

Ellie shook her head. "She's seriously demanding Kareem be expelled? This is BONKERS!"

Sam looked back up at Kareem's piece and gasped. "Ellie, that . . . that doesn't look like spray chalk."

Ellie looked up, too. "Holy mol-oney! You're right. It's totally real paint!" Then she grinned. "But you know what? It's the best one yet."

Sam considered the piece and nodded. "It is. It's the saddest, too."

"He signed it, right there." Cat Spencer herself appeared behind them, smiling smugly. "He's admitted it. It's over. Kareem's getting expelled. He may even go to jail. Defacing public property is a crime, you know."

All of Sam's anger at Cat seemed to explode in her chest at once.

"Why are you *like this?*" she yelled. Heads turned to look at her, and she went red, but she didn't stop. "Do you see what it says up there? Have you stopped, for even a second, to consider what any of the graffiti means or why someone might do this?"

"What's to consider?" Cat pointed at the school. "It's vandalism. It's not okay to paint whatever you want, wherever you want. Your cousin is going to get in big trouble. My father already talked to the principal, demanding he get kicked out."

"But look at what it *says*," said Sam. "Just read it."

"Um, Syria is burning?" Cat shrugged.

"And *nobody cares*, Cat. Nobody cares. Do you know what happened to Kareem's parents last night? The hospital they work in was bombed. BOMBED! And here you are complaining about some paint."

A small crowd gathered around them.

"Okayyy, but it has nothing to do with Allansdale or our school," said Cat tightly. "He's in America now, he can't just go painting on stuff like there aren't any rules here because *Syria* is always having wars."

"OH MY GOD. Cat Spencer, you are so . . . so clueless and self-centered. Syria isn't *always* having wars. Syria is a country with regular people, just like you and me, and we have to care about those people, we have to care about the world. Plus, Kareem isn't the only one who did the graffiti around town. I did it, too. If Kareem gets punished, so should I. If we're going to get in trouble for trying to tell people what's really happening in this world, then I'm fine with that. Seriously, Wake Up, Cat Spencer. Look Outside Your World!"

Sam locked arms with Ellie and walked away, feeling hundreds of eyes on them as they entered the school. She was angry. And sad. And worried. But, at the same time, she felt lighter than she had in ages. For the first time since fourth grade, Sam knew Cat Spencer was no longer her issue. She had said the things she had to say, in front of dozens of other students, and now she never had to think about nasty Cat Spencer ever again. Her burning cheeks slowly cooled.

"Sam!"

She turned around. Lucy was running after them, through the school's entryway.

"I saw the entire thing," panted Lucy. "Whoa. Cat's so . . . well, whatever. What can I do? How can I help?"

"We need to find Kareem," Sam said. Her phone vibrated. She pulled it out, hoping it was him. It wasn't. She looked at Ellie and Lucy. "Amari's in the art room."

"Why don't I look for Kareem in the park?" said Ellie. "We still have twenty minutes before the bell rings."

"Good idea," said Sam, looking at her phone again. "I think I need to talk to the principal. Lucy, can you go tell Amari what's happening? Let's meet at lunch."

Lucy and Ellie nodded and walked away, and Sam tensed as she walked to the principal's office. What was she going to say? She had to clearly explain what Kareem had been through. She had to tell her about the hospital and the bombing and Hassan. The graffiti, she'd leave for last. Kareem's future at the school depended on this. She took a deep breath and knocked.

"Principal Green?" Sam's voice quivered slightly. "It's Samira Sukkari."

"Oh, just the person I wanted to see. Come in."

CHAPTER 32

KAREEM

Kareem sat under a tree in the park and played with his phone. He checked his messages every few minutes. Nothing from Hassan. Six days and counting. His calls all went straight to voicemail. He tried Yusuf and George again. Same. A wave of fear washed over him. What if the mukhabarat had their phones? He texted his parents.

Kareem

Mama, Baba, are you okay?

Mama

We are fine. Will call you soon.

He checked the time. Seven thirty a.m.

People must be arriving at school by now. Band students, early-morning soccer practice, the principal, teachers preparing for their classes.

"Kareem!" A girl called his name. "Kareem!"

Kareem grabbed his bag, scrambling behind a hedge of bushes. It was Eleanora. She must have seen his piece. She walked past, calling out his name again. He felt bad hiding from her. He knew she would be on his side, but she'd still try to convince him to go home. There was no way he was going to his uncle's house. Not after what he had done.

Kareem had started spraying at four a.m. He'd finished just as the first rays of sun broke through the night sky. This was his largest piece yet. Normally, his body tingled from the adrenaline, but the morning air had been damp, and the smell of real paint had left him feeling a bit dizzy. He hadn't worked with real paint in a while. After he signed it, he'd collapsed right underneath the mural, sobbing until he ran out of tears. Then he had dried his face, collected his things, and run straight to the park, to wait for whatever would happen next.

As Eleanora's voice faded away, Kareem looked around at the rich greens of the treetops. Syria was mostly desert. The Baradā River, which ran through Damascus, had slowed to a mere trickle years ago, leaving the greenery ashen and thirsty. He admired a bunch of tulips. They looked like perfect wax molds, as if each one had been brightly painted: purple, yellow, orange. He reached out to touch them.

"They're soft," he said to himself. "They're beautiful."

Kareem thought of the bright red paint he'd used to write "Syria Is BURNING." The rest, he had sprayed in blue and black. The red had felt just right—the color of blood. People were losing their lives.

What have I done? How could I do this? To the clean walls in this perfect, beautiful town? With these pretty flowers? What did these people ever do to me?

Sure, they didn't really understand. But neither had he, before the revolution. He imagined all of Allansdale Middle School looking up at the mural, confused, asking, "What is Syria?" For all he knew, they'd think it was a school, like Cat. Kareem's eyes were heavy, his body weary. He tucked his backpack under his head and fell asleep.

He woke up an hour later. The park was empty. He jumped over the hedge and walked to school. When he reached the Red Cross building, he crouched behind a large tree and peered around it. Nearly a dozen parents were out in front of the school, along with the principal. Then Kareem caught a glimpse of his uncle and aunt among the adults. And police officers.

The POLICE.

Somehow, when he had concocted his plan, he had never actually pictured the police with their uniforms, cars, and siren lights. His heart pounded. He had imagined creating the piece, getting expelled, and then his mind had just skipped to the plane ride back to Syria. Did they even arrest kids in the United States? He looked at the school's social media posts and at Twitter. People were asking for him to be expelled. And arrested.

Yes, definitely arrested.

What do I do? They're going to tell Mama and Baba. Their hospital just got bombed and now they're going to find out that I . . . that I, Kareem Haddad, their son . . . graffitied the school. And got thrown out. And got sent to whatever Eleanora called it . . . juney.

Kareem ran back to the park, climbed through the hedge, and sat back down. He looked in his backpack. He had four cans of spray paint and about seven dollars.

He couldn't even make it to the next town with seven dollars.

He had to think. His phone's battery was down to five percent. Where could he go? If he went to Eleanora, he'd put her in the awkward position of having to lie. Sooner or later, they'd start combing the parks for him.

He left the park and walked down a back road that wound its way behind some stores. From there, he could get to the highway, where he'd once seen people camping out under the columns. Nobody would look for him there.

CHAPTER 33

SAMIRA

Sam ran up to the art room. Amari, Ellie, and Lucy were sitting around a table whispering when she burst in.

"Sam!" said Amari. "That was seriously the coolest piece of art I've ever seen. And it's *your* cousin who's doing all this! Did you know?"

"Not the whole time," Sam said, glancing at Ellie.

"I knew," said Ellie. "But we've both been in on it for a little while now."

"Legit," said Amari, shaking his head in amazement. "That's legit."

"Has anybody seen Kareem yet?" Sam said. "Or heard from him?"

"Nope," said Ellie, her brow furrowing. "I couldn't find him in the park. I've been calling and texting, but he's not answering. What happened in the office?"

"It's not good. Kareem's in big trouble."

"What do you mean?" asked Ellie.

"I mean, I explained the whole thing to Mrs. Green, and she sort of got it. She feels bad for him, but she said parents are calling and demanding that Kareem get expelled and that graffitiing public property is a crime. I don't know what's going to happen."

Her mind was racing. They needed to do something to convince the parents, the whole town, that what Kareem had done wasn't a crime. Or if it *was* a crime, that he'd had to do it. That it was okay.

The bell rang.

"We'd better go to class," said Lucy.

"Okay, we'll talk more at lunch," said Sam. "We have to come up with a plan."

◊

Sam took a seat at Kareem and Ellie's table in the cafeteria. Within minutes, Amari and Lucy joined them. They'd all texted each other nonstop all morning—underneath their desks, in the bathroom, behind their books. Amari had also doubled down on his pro-graffiti posts, which were getting likes and reposts, but Cat was upping the stakes with the new hashtags: #GraffitiIsACrime and #ExpelKareem.

Sam wondered what her parents were going to do. Would they tell Kareem's parents? She knew her dad would go ballistic when he saw the graffiti on the school.

"Did you guys see #ExpelKareem?" asked Sam.

Amari reached out and patted her arm, looking her in the eyes. "We'll figure it out," he said. "They can't expel Kareem!"

Sam wanted to believe him that they'd find a solution, but Cat had somehow managed to get a lot of people to re-share her stupid hashtags. People who knew nothing about Syria, or Kareem, or what was happening outside their small town.

"Hey, what are you weirdos up to?" asked Dylan, his voice hesitant. He stood next to their table holding a tray of food, shifting his weight from foot to foot. To Amari he said, "Why are you sitting over here?"

Sam looked up at Dylan, furious. He was so clueless. "We're taking on your sister," she said. "So unless you're in, we need to get to work."

"You guys are taking on my sister?" he repeated incredulously. "Why?"

"Because she's trying to get Kareem in trouble, but she has no idea what's really going on," said Amari, looking directly at Dylan. "She doesn't get it. She doesn't get why he's been doing this, or why it's important. Not sure why she cares, honestly—I guess she's just not happy unless she's making somebody miserable."

Dylan looked down at his feet, then said quietly, "She needs to stop bullying people. I'm so sick of it."

For a second, Sam actually thought Dylan might cry. She knew they bickered a lot, but she'd never thought about what it must be like to be Cat Spencer's sibling.

Dylan sat down next to Lucy. "I'm in."

Sam thought of what he had just said—Cat needed to stop bullying. They had to force her to end her social media offensive. Twitter, the school blog. All of it. But how could they really bring it? Hashtags weren't doing it anymore. They needed to win the media battle once and for all.

"I got it!" she blurted, startling even herself. "Cat started a social media war, right? She's calling Kareem's work vandalism. We just need to turn the story around. We have to tag the story straight."

Amari nodded thoughtfully. "I like that. Tagging the story straight." He gave her a fist bump. "Listen to this lady. She knows what she's talking about!"

"I don't get it," Dylan said.

"The only way to tell the real story is . . . with graffiti."

Amari smiled. So did Ellie. Lucy and Dylan looked at the others, wide-eyed.

"So Kareem's about to get in trouble for the graffiti," Dylan said. "And you're saying that to fix it, we have to do MORE graffiti?"

"Yep," said Sam confidently. "That's the only way to prove it isn't vandalism. We have to get through to people that what Kareem did is *activism*. He had to let people know what's happening and to try to make them care. It's sort of what we've been doing already, but on a bigger and more targeted scale."

She paused to take a breath, then looked around the table seriously. "But the thing is . . . we have to sign, and with our real names. If Kareem gets in trouble, we all get in trouble. If he gets expelled, so do we. If Kareem is a vandal, then so are we."

Amari and Ellie's eyes widened. They looked at each other. And then, slowly, both nodded.

"This girl knows what she's talking about!" yelled Amari as he jumped up, nearly twirling with excitement.

Kids turned to look at them.

"Amari, too loud," said Ellie, gesturing for him to sit.

"Oh, sorry," he whispered. "People, this girl is the GOAT. The REAL DEAL. She knows how to start a revolution."

Sam giggled at his enthusiasm. "Okay, okay, calm down."

"Sam, I don't know," said Lucy. She shifted in her seat and struggled to look Sam in the eyes. "I can't get expelled. My parents will murder me."

"We're only using spray chalk. We can use that to our advantage." Sam put on her most innocent expression. "You're going to expel us for playing with chalk? Who plays with chalk other than kids?"

She could tell her attempt to alleviate their fears hadn't worked. For the first time in ages, Sam knew what she needed to do. But they looked really scared, and she knew exactly how that felt. It wasn't fair to make them do this. They weren't ready. She hadn't been ready either, before.

"Okay, listen, neither of you were part of this before, so it doesn't make sense for you to add your names. But Ellie and I have to add our names."

She looked to her best friend for confirmation. Ellie nodded.

"Me too," said Amari. "I'm so in."

Sam smiled.

"How about we combine our names," suggested Amari. "Like . . . SaKamaLi? Or Karamelam? And *then* sign Sam, Amari, Ellie, and Kareem?"

Sam thought of the two options. But they needed something easier. Their initials were K-S-A-E. She ran through permutations of the letters in her head. "Oh! How about SAKE!" she said with a big smile. "Samira, Amari, Kareem, Ellie. We can tag, 'For Syria's SAKE, We Stand With Kareem.' Then we can sign our full names."

Amari nodded. "Or how about, 'For Freedom's SAKE,' and then sign our names."

"That's brilliant, you guys," said Lucy. "I'll help spray-paint, at least. I mean, spray chalk."

"Me too," added Dylan. "I can spray."

"Yes, chalk," said Sam, nodding. "That would be awesome, Lucy. Thanks, Dylan. So we have to split up and tag everywhere, everything. We need all of Allansdale to read these messages."

They all nodded.

"So is that what we're spraying—'For Syria's SAKE, We Stand With Kareem'?" asked Dylan. "And then your names?"

"Well, we have to sign all of them SAKE, but we should tag different messages," Amari said. "The point is to defend

Kareem and graffiti. Oh, and Syria, so that people understand that this was always about something bigger."

He opened a blank page on his phone's notes app, typed a list, then showed the group.

#SyriaIsBurning

#HelpSyria

#WeStandWithKareem

#WeStandWithSyria

#GraffitiIsActivism

#ForFreedomsSAKE

"Am I missing anything?" he asked.

Lucy looked at Sam hopefully. "How about 'Spirit Squad for Syria'?"

Sam smiled. "Perfect."

Amari added it, then sent everyone the list.

"Okay, let's go," said Sam, standing.

"Wait, aren't we doing this after school?" asked Lucy, sounding confused.

"Nope, we're doing it now," said Sam, looking at everybody. "We should split up into groups."

"I'll babysit Dylan," said Amari, nudging his friend.

Dylan scowled at him and then smiled sheepishly. "Probably a good idea. I've never graffitied before."

"Great," said Sam. "Lucy, why don't you tag with Ellie, and I'll go on my own. First, Ellie and I will get the spray chalk from Ellie's house. Let's meet in half an hour, at the top of the park. Try to leave from different exits if you can. I'll exit from the field."

The gang all nodded and dispersed.

Sam exited out of the gym and onto a side street. No one stopped her. She walked toward Ellie's house, thinking about how she had just ditched school and was about to go on a tagging spree with no wingman. The others all had partners, but she wanted to tag alone. No one to lean on, no one to hide behind. It felt perfect. She was doing exactly what she needed to do. She was going to tell everybody what was happening in Syria, and she was going to take care of her cousin.

Ellie ran up behind Sam and hooked her arm into hers. They looked at each other, took a deep breath, and walked in silence for a few minutes, each of them deep in thought. Now they just needed to find Kareem.

CHAPTER 34

KAREEM

Kareem opened his eyes. He had fallen asleep against a column of the freeway underpass. He'd tried to keep warm with his jacket and backpack, but it was no use. His clothes were damp from the night air, and he couldn't stop shivering. It was the middle of the night, but he wasn't sure what time it was; his phone battery had run out hours ago. He had spent all of yesterday hiding, into the night, listening to sirens, knowing that his cousin and aunt and uncle were probably out there looking for him. For the first time, he felt what it was like to *really* be alone. No phone, no home, no family around him.

He needed to move. He got up and brushed the wet gravel off his pants, planning to head back to the enclave in the park. At least it was a little more comfortable. He would feel safer there as well. The underpass was spooky and dark and dreary. He had already met a dozen rats and an opossum, which had stared him down until he threw a stick at it.

His stomach grumbled. He couldn't remember ever being this hungry, not even during Ramadan. In Ramadan, he would have broken his fast hours ago. He was cold and hungry and angry and tired and confused and scared. And he had no idea what to do.

He approached the main road and walked up the hill. When he reached the top, he stopped. There was chalk all over the ground.

"Shoo hada?" he said out loud. "What is this?"

Kareem walked slowly down the block, keeping his gaze fixed on the road in front of him. Block after block had been tagged. Hashtags for Syria, hashtags for him, hashtags about freedom. #HelpSyria; #WeStandWithKareem; #GraffitiIsActivism. For Syria's SAKE, We Stand With Kareem. He rubbed his eyes. Was he dreaming?

The hashtags were signed. All of them. SAKE: Samira Sukkari, Amari Light, Kareem Haddad, Eleanora Gold. Their full names, right there, for all to see.

SAKE. Ha. That's clever. And she signed it. Her entire name. Samira.

Kareem smiled. He kept his head down, reading the hashtags as he walked past the park. On every block, new tags appeared. #SpiritSquadforSyria. They were in different scripts in different people's writing. As he walked, he said each new one out loud.

#KareemCOMEHOME! #DonateforSyria
#SupportKareem #FreedomforSyria

They did this for me?

He was so fixated on the tags that he barely noticed the tears streaming down his face. He had been so angry—angry at what was happening in Syria, angry that he was so far away, angry that his friends might be in trouble, angry at Samira and Eleanora too, that they didn't really get it. But here they were, in bright pink and silver and orange and green and purple, signing their names, their full names, completely exposed, for all to see. Their names were right next to his.

He looked up and realized he was standing outside his aunt and uncle's house. The tags had led him home. Something in his body relaxed.

The world wasn't fair. He was so scared for his friends and his parents. But now he was certain of one thing—Eleanora and Samira did care. They were showing him that they supported him, that they understood why he'd done what he did. He already regretted doing it. But that piece was inside him and it had to come out. Sam and Ellie understood that.

He opened the front door. He heard footsteps pounding immediately and as soon as he stepped inside, Samira and Eleanora tackled him, hugging him tightly. Tant Ranya rushed into the foyer right behind them. She gave Kareem a hug as well. She had her phone in her hand.

"Alhamdulillah, alhamdulillah, you're okay. I have to call your uncle. He's out looking for you."

"Kareem, we've been so worried," said Sam. Her pants were covered in magenta and silver. She even had chalk in her hair.

"We were looking for you all night." Ellie's voice cracked. She looked close to tears.

Kareem closed his eyes and breathed in.

"I'm sorry," he said. "I'm sorry, Tant Ranya. I'm sorry. I just wanted to go home. To Syria, I mean. I wanted to get kicked out of school so that I could go back. I didn't really . . . I didn't really think it through."

"We know, Kareem," said Sam. "We're just so happy you're okay."

Kareem wasn't sure what to say. He wanted to apologize over and over again, but he knew apologies wouldn't count for much right now. Not after he'd put them through a night of hell. Tant Ranya was already talking into the phone, turning away from them briefly to tell his uncle that he was home safe.

"Kareem," said Ellie. "We really do want to help. We want to do something for you, and for Syria."

A tear ran down Kareem's cheek. "I saw."

"You saw?" said Sam.

"The sidewalk graffiti. It's all over town."

"Oh yeah, there's a new Spirit Squad in town," she said, smiling. "They've been shared so many times, too."

"Thanks, Samira." He wiped his eyes and smiled back. "I couldn't believe it." He paused. "I guess it's the reason I came back. The hashtags led me here. It's like they were telling me it was okay to come . . . home."

He gave Sam and Ellie big hugs.

"I don't know what's going to happen at school, though," said Sam. "A bunch of people are talking about you getting expelled."

"I just hope I don't get arrested."

A car pulled into the driveway.

"Baba is home," Sam said, patting Kareem's back. "First you need to get through him."

Moments later, the front door opened.

"Alhamdulillah . . . ya Rab!" Khalo Ahmed yelled, throwing his arms in the air. He picked Kareem up and hugged him, then said into his phone, "He's here, Sheriff Gold. Come right over."

Khalo Ahmed hung up and pushed Kareem away to get a look at him. "Habibi, are you okay? I was about to call your parents. I didn't even know how I was going to tell them."

Kareem's uncle looked worn down and disheveled. His hair was a mess, and his shirt was untucked and unbuttoned at the top. Kareem had never seen him like this.

"Khalo, please don't tell them," Kareem pleaded. "Please don't. Please. I'm sorry. I'm so sorry I did this. I messed up. I shouldn't have graffitied the school. I was just . . . so . . . so . . . mad. And scared. And . . . please don't tell them, Khalo. I'm so sorry."

Tears trickled down Khalo Ahmed's face as he pulled Kareem back into a hug and held him tightly. "I know, albi. I know. We'll figure it out."

When Khalo Ahmed finally let go, Kareem wiped his face with his sleeve, took his phone from his pocket, and plugged it into the communal living room charger.

"Ahh, so that is why we couldn't get ahold of you," said Khalo Ahmed.

"It died last night." Kareem looked at his uncle apologetically. "I'm sorry, Khalo."

As soon as it had charged a moment, Kareem's phone lit up and started vibrating frantically.

"Ahh, there you go, all our messages, Kareem," said Khalo Ahmed. He sat at the kitchen table and breathed a big sigh of relief, while Tant Ranya prepared tea for them. "Listen, we're not done yet, Kareem. After I've recovered from the last few hours, we need to talk."

Kareem nodded and went to check his phone. "My Twitter feed is lighting up," he said to Sam and Eleanora. "And . . ." He opened his messages and saw a name that made him jump up and down.

"It's Hassan! He texted!" Kareem read the messages, his eyes glistening. "He's fine! He's in Beirut. I guess his parents made him leave, too." He typed a response and said, "He's okay, he's okay."

Sam and Ellie were smiling and crying with him. Hassan was okay. Kareem's parents were okay. Tomorrow, he would face the principal and the rest of the school. But all of that was beside the point. His family was near him, and Hassan was okay. That was all that mattered.

CHAPTER 35

SAMĪRA

Sam and Amari marched next to one another, each of them holding a megaphone in their free hand. Ellie and Layla linked arms to Sam's left, while Lucy linked arms with Amari to his right. In front of them, Dylan and Kareem marched with a banner that read HELP SYRIA NOW in a large, blocky script. Below it, in slightly smaller script: WE MUST CARE.

"Syria matters," Amari chanted over his megaphone.

"Yes, we care!" responded the throng of denim-clad walkers, many of whom held handmade signs.

Sam couldn't believe she had made this happen, but she'd put her punishment time to good use. Though her parents had convinced the school's administration not to expel anyone, Sam, Kareem, and Ellie had all been suspended for a week and had been given thirty hours of community service. They'd spent that time cleaning the town's graffiti and painting over Kareem's mural. And at Sam's urging, they'd brainstormed as they worked.

Their hushed planning continued into a month of after-school detentions. Amari had joined them after practically throwing a temper tantrum for not also being suspended. He pestered Principal Green for days, arguing he'd aided and abetted as the social media mastermind and was just as responsible for the graffiti spree as the others. Eventually, the principal added him to the detention crew just to get him off her back.

It had been during those after-school detentions that Sam and Amari came up with the idea for JEANS—the Justice, Equality & Action Now Squad. They decided JEANS would hold activities, teach-ins, and fundraisers every few months on a designated issue, starting with Syria. Kareem and her parents led a teach-in at the school, where they explained what was happening in Syria. Their impassioned account had mobilized the entire school to join a walkathon to raise money for Syrian hospitals.

"Syria matters," Amari chanted.

"Yes, we care!" the marchers responded.

Sam admired the sea of jean jackets around her. She made eye contact with her dad and mom, who were marching next to Sheriff Gold a few rows behind her, holding signs that read SYRIA DESERVES TO BE FREE. She smiled. She never thought she would lead a walkathon about Syria in Allansdale, of all places. Her dad winked at her, and Sam smiled back. When she'd told her parents about JEANS and how she'd organized a fundraising march for Syria, their anger had disappeared almost instantly. They told her that they had never been so proud. In that moment, Sam thought the world had flipped upside down.

"Syria matters!" Amari held the megaphone in his right hand, the patched arm of his jean jacket pumping high into the air as the crowd called back to him. Samira laughed as he tried to break out some dance moves.

Amari grinned and mouthed, "Time for the new chant?"

Sam nodded. They'd agreed they would take turns leading the chants. Sam had practiced a new one the night before with SAKE, and she was definitely ready for its debut.

"Show me what JUSTICE looks like," Sam yelled.

"This is what justice looks like," she heard Ellie and Layla yell back. She loved having them both next to her, walking in solidarity. Before, she could never imagine them both by her side. But here they were, arms linked, chanting as one.

"Show me what EQUALITY looks like!"

"This is what equality looks like," she heard Kareem and Dylan call back.

Kareem turned around and beamed at Sam, just as Sam called out: "Show me what ACTION looks like!"

By now, the whole crowd had caught on and responded as one, as Sam cycled back through the JEANS chant again. When she reached the NOW, she looked at Amari, and together, they led the part.

SAM: When do we want it?
AMARI: Now!

SAM and AMARI TOGETHER: When do we want it?
CROWD: NOW!

As everyone shouted NOW in unison, Sam felt as though she was flying high above the crowd, watching a sea of JEANS-wearing students who suddenly cared, who were seeing something beyond the walled world of their school. The crowd turned the corner and walked past the field toward the main street. Sam took in a deep breath and smiled. As the NOW echoed through the crowd, she caught a glimpse of Cat, Avery, and a few other Spirit Squad stragglers huddled together on the field, pretending not to notice the people marching past. Dylan had tried to convince his sister to join the rally, but she'd only responded with: "When monkeys fly." Sam couldn't understand why she was so stubbornly opposed to it all. Sam didn't know why the spray chalk had caused her to go so ballistic, but as she chanted together with her new squad, she knew it was no longer important. And neither was Cat Spencer.

During a lull in the call-and-response, Sam called out to Kareem and pointed to the gym on the other side of the field. "Over there. That wall."

He followed her finger, smiled, and gave her a thumbs-up. Over the last few weeks, JEANS had led a campaign demanding the school acknowledge that graffiti wasn't merely an act of vandalism but also one of activism. Sam wanted everyone to understand why Kareem had done what he did and why they had chosen to stand by him.

After weeks of petitions and articles in the school newspaper, the administration finally capitulated and even announced an annual, *sanctioned* graffiti competition. The gym's wall had been designated as the prize canvas. After the anonymous entries were submitted and the entire student body voted, SAKE's was declared the winner. Sam, Kareem, Amari, and Ellie would create their mural over the summer to have it ready for the new school year.

Sam knew sanctioned graffiti changed the nature of graffiti in general. But, for now, it was a step. It was hard for four kids in Allansdale to change the world. But it was a start. She understood more than ever that even if the world wasn't paying attention, it didn't mean it wasn't happening. Sometimes, she couldn't handle the sadness, but it didn't mean she could ignore the truth. She had to try.

Sam chanted and raised her megaphone into the air. JEANS was now walking toward the town's square, to tell all of Allansdale that Syria mattered, and that this particular group of people cared. Her friends' letters were bold and clear, announcing their unwavering presence. Layla was still her fun, confident cursive. Amari glowed in his 1980s subway-style graffiti letters. Ellie's were still boxy, crisp, and quirky in their high-reaching stance. Lucy's were sweet, bubbly, and welcoming. And Sam was so happy they were here with her—bright and loyal and beautiful.

As for Kareem, his letters remained strident, if a bit wilted and sad and scared. But they were no longer always struck through with aggressive, thick, Sharpie lines. When he was worried, the old Kareem would sometimes reappear, but overall, his font was a beautiful, bold Arabic script, more open than before.

Most importantly, Sam could finally see her own letters. Yes, they were a little crooked, and they sometimes slouched under the weight of the world around her, but they were strong. English letters, with an Arabesque flair, and for the first time in years, clear, tall, and confident.

CHAPTER 36

KAREEM

Kareem stood on the second to top rung of the ladder, in front of the gym's beige wall. Using his arms for balance, he straightened his tall, thin frame. He pressed one hand to the wall, careful not to touch any wet paint, and drew a curved semicircle in the left upper quadrant. Below him, Ellie used a paint pen to create crisp lines around the silhouette of children holding hands around the globe. A little farther along, Sam was high up another ladder finishing the letters above the mural. Down on the ground, Layla, Lucy, and Amari were opening the other cans of paint.

"Samira, your letters are tilted," called Layla.

Kareem leaned back a little to look at them. Layla was right, but they were more real this way. It looked perfect.

Sam stuck her tongue out. "Have you considered that maybe *you're* tilted, Layla?"

At the base of the ladder, Layla held up a brush soaked with bright orange paint and pretended to aim it at Sam. "I'm a pretty straight shot."

"Don't you dare, Layla Hamdan, don't you dare!"

Kareem laughed as Sam scurried down her ladder and ran for a bucket of green paint.

"PAINT WAR!" yelled Amari, flinging blue at Ellie and Kareem.

They scrambled off their ladders and charged for the other buckets. Kareem plunged his brush into the orange and took aim at Amari right as Sam's dad pulled up in front of the playground. Kareem froze.

"You just finished a month of detention *and* a one-week suspension," Khalo Ahmed's voice rang over their squeals. "You know Principal Green is inside, don't you?"

"Everybody, TRUCE!" Sam slowly placed her soaked brush on the brush pan. "Brushes down!"

Kareem put his down, too. He was happy to see his uncle. Even though Sam's parents weren't *his* parents, they were family. New explosions had gone off in Damascus in the last few weeks, and that had sent Kareem spiraling, but he was learning not to spiral alone. It helped to know Hassan was safe in Beirut. Hassan had also told him that Ramy was Spray Man, but Ramy had been released a few weeks ago. Ever since Ramy's arrest, Yusuf and George had been laying low.

But the revolution was getting more dangerous every day, and his parents' hospital was in the middle of it all. Not only were they taking care of the wounded, but their hospital had been hit a few times. Kareem spent many sleepless nights worrying about them—but it was comforting to be surrounded by people who cared.

Today he had an appointment with a lawyer about an asylum application. He wasn't sure how he felt about it. He didn't want to give up on Syria, and applying for asylum somehow felt like a betrayal. He still desperately wanted to go back home to his old life, but his parents had convinced him that for now, this was the best course of action. Asylum meant he couldn't go home yet because it was too dangerous. He needed the United States to accept him as a refugee.

Kareem stood back with the others and surveyed their mural. At first, he'd scoffed at the idea of legal, school-approved graffiti. Permission went against the soul of street art. But when Ellie and Samira had shown him and Amari their sketch, he knew he wanted to be a part of it.

Kareem's painted globe was ringed by Ellie's shadowy children. Syria was right at the center. Around the top, Sam had written in cursive: *When We Care Together; When We Stand Together.* Below, in bold block letters, she'd put: WE WILL CHANGE THE WORLD!

Amari snapped a few pictures of the mural and posted it on the JEANS website and Twitter. Along with the walkathon and weekly bake sales, they'd already raised more than $3,000 for Syrian hospitals and refugees.

"Kareem," his uncle called. "We're going to be late."

Sam turned to Kareem and smiled. "Before you go, we need to sign it. And I think you should do it."

Kareem took the thick paint marker he'd used on the globe's detailing. "Okay, what should I write?"

"How about SAKE?" suggested Ellie. "I mean, it *is* our signature."

"I like that." Kareem approached the wall, then paused. "How about we use . . ." He added the signature, then turned around to show them. ". . . this one."

For Freedom's Sake.

The group admired the mural together.

"Group hug!" yelled Lucy as they all dog-piled onto Kareem.

"Yes, it's perfect," Sam said, putting her arm around Kareem as he made his way out of the friend pile.

"Kareem!" his uncle called again. "Come on. It's time to go."

Kareem put the paint marker in his pocket and jogged to the car. The world was far from perfect, but this mural, this signature, his friends, his family—they made it all a little better. He couldn't join the revolution from Allansdale, but for now, he could be a different type of activist. Maybe he could still make a difference. He hopped into the car and texted his parents. He messaged them a few times a day now and they did their best to respond right away. They had even started talking about meeting in Turkey once his immigration papers were done, and that thought kept Kareem going.

He sat back and admired the red and yellow leaves of the trees. He'd never seen these colors before. He missed Damascus. So much that his heart sometimes ached. He looked at his uncle and smiled. Sabah Fakhri played over the car's speakers. "Ya Mal el-Sham." His ode to Damascus. Kareem had heard the song a million times. He always thought it was corny—how his parents sang it with friends, swaying, their eyes closed, entranced. But now he understood. Syria was inside him, too. It was in his uncle. It was even in Samira. In their memories. In their stories and songs. He closed his eyes and felt the breeze on his face. For the first time, he understood every word.

> *Oh treasure of Damascus, come, my treasure*
> *It has been so long, come to me, my beauty.*
>
> *The most beautiful time I spent with you.*
> *You promised me and you made a pact with me*
> *You won't forget me and I won't forget you.*
> *No matter how many nights or years you are absent.*
>
> *Oh treasure of Damascus, come, my treasure*
> *It has been so long, come to me, my beauty.*

The time gets longer and longer
I won't change and I won't waver

I miss you, oh, the light of my eyes.
I miss you, oh, the light of my eyes.
So that we repeat the beginning
So that we repeat the beginning—come back.

Oh treasure of Damascus, come, my treasure

Author's Note

If you told Syrians in the early months of 2011 that a war would tear their country apart, they would not have believed you. Syria was a peaceful, safe country. It was a place where kids were allowed to play unsupervised in their neighborhood, even at night. War was not something that Syrians ever thought about, let alone expected to experience in their lifetime.

I wrote this book not to write about war or refugees. I wanted to write about the beginning. Before the devastation and the deaths and the refugees, there was a period of hope, a moment that captured the hearts and imagination of the Arab world. It was a moment when Arabs—Syrians, Egyptians, Yemenis, Tunisians, and so many others—believed change was possible, that a new future was possible. Syrians, Egyptians, Yemenis, Tunisians imagined their countries, free of corruption, free of dictatorship, and free of fear. It was a world where graffiti was possible, where the will of the people finally mattered.

The truth is, the story of Syria's war over the last decade is both tragic and complicated.

Unfortunately, Syria's revolution does not have a happy ending. As more and more violence erupted, the revolution slowly morphed into a war. By the end of 2012, very little in Syria looked peaceful. Some people still called it a revolution. Some called it a civil war, which is a war waged between different groups in the same country. Others, like me, believed "civil war" was too simple a description. In reality, the war extended beyond Syria's borders. More countries in the region got involved—like Iran, Saudi Arabia, and Turkey—as did bigger countries such as Russia, China, and the United States.

The Syrian war created the worst humanitarian crisis since World War II, with more than 400,000 deaths, 5.5 million refugees displaced around the world, and 6 million people displaced internally. (A refugee is a person who is forced to flee their country because of war, violence, or a fear of being persecuted. An internally displaced person is someone who has been forced to flee their home, but who finds safety elsewhere within their own country.)

Building new countries is not easy. Even the revolutions in Egypt and other Arab countries took strange turns. But just because a country's revolution does not succeed, it does not mean that its people do not still yearn for freedom. After all, history is a long, long story. And it is not over.

This book is a work of fiction, but some of its events and characters are based on real incidents and people. Here are some facts and anecdotes you might find interesting after reading *Tagging Freedom*.

The Story of the Tunisian Vegetable Seller

Twenty-six-year-old Mohamed Bouazizi was a vegetable seller in the small Tunisian town of Sidi Bouzid. On December 17, 2010, Mohamed loaded his wheelbarrow with produce he'd procured the night before with a month's salary and headed to the local market.

Mohamed was often harassed by local authorities because he could not afford to pay the bribes police officers demanded of street sellers. That day was no different. When he couldn't pay the bribe, an officer publicly scolded him, toppled his wheelbarrow, and confiscated his produce and scales.

It wasn't the first time this had happened to Mohamed, but this time he'd had enough. He went to the governor's office to complain and retrieve his belongings. When the authorities wouldn't see him, Mohamed stood in the center of the city square and allegedly screamed, "How do you expect me to make a living?"

Then he set himself on fire.

Mohamed was taken to the hospital, and hundreds of protesters flooded the city square in solidarity. He wasn't the only one fed up with the corruption. Within ten days, protests had spread to the capital and across the entire country. President Zine al-Abidine Ben Ali, who had ruled Tunisia for more than two decades, tried everything to quell the unrest. He blamed the protesters and imprisoned them, promised new jobs, fired ministers, and promised reforms. But as the days passed, more and more people joined the protests, until the country was on fire.

On January 14, less than a month later, Ben Ali left on a plane headed for Malta. Instead, he landed in Saudi Arabia, where he resigned. In the end, an extreme act of desperation from a local vegetable seller inadvertently set off a revolution that led not only to the ousting of a dictator but eventually to revolutions across the Arab world.

The Story of the Egyptian Revolution

People across the Arab world could relate to Mohamed's story. They were tired of their own dictators and the rampant corruption that made it so hard to earn a living. The fact that they had the highest youth populations along with the highest rates of unemployment made it ripe for unrest.

After Tunisia ousted its dictator, it was Egypt's turn. Just a week later, on January 25, Egypt revolted. As the Arab world's most populous country (population 85 million), Egypt's revolution caught the entire Arab world's attention.

The scenes were breathtaking. Hundreds of thousands—some even said millions—gathered in Tahrir Square in Egypt's capital, Cairo, to demand an end to corruption and police brutality, and calling for President Hosni Mubarak to step down. People chanted and waved Egyptian flags.

For seventeen days straight, Egyptians of all ages showed up. Each day, their numbers swelled.

Mubarak eventually stepped down on February 11, 2011.

Al Sha'ab Youreed Isqaat al Nizam

"Al Sha'ab Youreed Isqaat al Nizam" or "The people want the downfall of the government" became the most popular chant of the Egyptian revolution. It then became the most popular chant of *all* the Arab revolutions, which took place in Libya, Yemen, and Bahrain. Major protests also occurred in Morocco, Iraq, Jordan, Algeria, Lebanon, Kuwait, Oman, and Sudan.

The term "the Arab Spring" was used by western commentators to describe these revolutions.

It was not used in the Arab world.

Hamza al-Khateeb

The story of the boys from the southern Syrian town of Dara'a is true.

Hamza al-Khateeb was thirteen years old when he was detained in Syria's southern town of Dara'a for attending a protest with his family. He died in custody, and his story spread on Facebook and Twitter and was covered by the Arab media.

His death led to outrage and protests across Syria. He eventually became a symbol of the Syrian revolution, just like Mohamed Bouazizi had in Tunisia.

Graffiti in Syria

Before the revolution, graffiti did not exist in Syria. If expressing your political opinions in public was not an option, writing them on walls was unimaginable. The boys from Dara'a, who were aged between ten and fifteen, were mostly inspired by spray-painted walls in Egypt and Tunisia they'd seen on television. They painted *It's your turn, Doctor* on their school, referring to Syrian president Bashar al-Assad, who had trained as an ophthalmologist in the UK.

The boys were all arrested. Some were beaten and kept in prison for weeks.

As the revolution continued, more and more graffiti appeared around Syria. The character of Ramy was named after one of the country's most famous graffiti artists, Nour Hatem Zahra, who was nicknamed Spray Man. Not only did he and his friends tag messages of freedom around Damascus, Zahra helped organize protests, hide those wanted by the mukhabarat, and get medical supplies and care to injured people who feared going to a hospital.

Nour Hatem Zahra was arrested once, then released. Together with his friends, he created Freedom Graffiti Week on Facebook. On April 29, 2012, he was shot while graffitiing around the capital.

He died from his injuries.

Doctors and Hospitals in Syria

In *Tagging Freedom*, Kareem's parents stay behind in Syria as doctors and, during the course of the book, their hospital is hit by a bomb. Doctors in Syria had some of the most difficult jobs during the revolution and war. In wartime, different sides are expected to abide by certain rules that are meant to protect civilians. These rules were set after World War II and are collectively referred to as the Geneva Convention. According to Article 19 of the 1949 Geneva Convention, "Fixed establishments and mobile medical units of the Medical Service may in no circumstances be attacked, but shall at all times be respected and protected by the Parties to the conflict."

Throughout the revolution and then the war, the Syrian and Russian military frequently targeted hospitals, like the one where Kareem's parents would have worked, to try to weaken the opposition. Many doctors fled the war and violence, but those who stayed faced a lot of danger as they tried to help civilians during the war. Eventually, the doctors built secret hospitals, many of them underground, so they could evade such attacks. A hospital like that of Kareem's parents would probably not have faced missiles or explosions in the first months of the revolution; that came later. Many doctors who stayed to help in Syria often took breaks from the conflict and stress by heading to nearby countries, like Turkey or Lebanon. Sometimes those doctors would also visit their families during that time, since they had sent them to live in neighboring cities or countries to make sure they were safe.

Glossary of Terms

ARABIC WORDS USED IN THIS BOOK

GENERAL WORDS

Adhan: call to prayer

Allah: the word for "God" in Arabic, used by Muslims, Christians, and other religious groups who believe in God and speak Arabic

Allah Sattar: God Protected

Allah Yustor: God Protects

Ana kaman: Me too!

Bas: That's all, or Enough

Habibi: My love, my dear. Used among friends, casually, and for loved ones, more intimately.

Houriyeh: freedom

Ihtiram nafsak: Respect yourself

Insha'Allah: God Willing

Insha'Allah Khair: May God Will Good; or, May God Bring Goodness

Iskoutey: Be quiet, or Shut up. Can be said playfully.

Khawana: traitors

Nadi: rec club or community center that has fields, swimming pools, and cafes

Shiffit, iltilak: You see, I told you. "Shiffit" means "You see." "Iltilak" means "I told you."

Shtatilak or **Shtatilik:** I missed you (he or she); in a Syrian dialect.

Yalla: Used often, it means "let's go." Yalla, boys.

Wallahi: I swear to God.

FAMILY RELATIONS

Amo: Paternal uncle, or uncle from the father's side. Also used for family friends and acquaintances. Can informally be used by children to address anybody older than them, even, say, a taxi driver or a salesperson. Similarly, *Amto* is used as paternal aunt, or aunt from the father's side.

Jiddo: grandfather

Khalo: term for maternal uncle, or uncle from the mother's side

Khalto: maternal aunt, or aunt from the mother's side

Tant: A French word that's used by Arabs. It is the equivalent of "aunt," usually used for those who are not actual relatives.

Teta: grandmother

POLITICAL WORDS

Mukhabarat: the secret police
Shabiha: Technically it translates to "ghosts," but is used
to refer to regime thugs who often intimidate protesters
through violence.

PHRASES

Houriyeh Al'an: Freedom Now
Ma raha itrikak: I'm not going to leave you (alone).
Tawley balik: Calm down. In this construction, it is said to
a girl.
Ya shabab: Hey, youth. "Ya," used before a word, is like
saying, "Hey, you." Ya, [name of person]. Ya, habibi—hey
you, love.

CHANTS

Allah, Souriyah, Houriyah ou Bas: God, Syria, Freedom Only
Al Sha'ab Youreed Isqaat al Nizam: The people want to
bring down the government.
Yalla, Irhal, ya Bashar: Yalla, Leave Bashar

"Ya Mal el-Sham" by Sabah Fakhri
Translated by Mona Roumani

Oh treasure of Damascus, come, my treasure
It has been so long, come to me, my beauty.

The most beautiful time I spent with you.
You promised me and you made a pact with me
You won't forget me and I won't forget you.
No matter how many nights or years you are absent.

Oh treasure of Damascus, come, my treasure
It has been so long, come to me, my beauty.

The time gets longer and longer
I won't change and I won't waver

I miss you, oh, the light of my eyes.
I miss you, oh, the light of my eyes.
So that we repeat the beginning
So that we repeat the beginning—come back.

Oh treasure of Damascus, come, my treasure
It has been so long, come to me, my beauty.

Acknowledgments

As with a child, it takes a village to raise a book. And this village is one of the most generous and most beautiful communities I've ever been a part of.

Brent Taylor, I'm so blessed to work with such an amazing agent. Thank you for choosing *Tagging Freedom* from your slush pile and then championing it all the way to the finish line. Your patience, accessibility, guidance, and support have meant the world to me.

To Suzy Capozzi, thank you for loving this story and my characters as much as I do and for bringing *Tagging Freedom* to the world. I am forever grateful for your support and vision. Thank you to Melissa Farris, Renee Yewdaev, Diane Joao, Sandy Noman, Dan Denning, Jenny Lu, and so many others who helped put this book together.

I am grateful to so many amazing women who have helped me along this writing journey. Writing alongside these smart, creative women—and among so many other POC authors and allies—has made me feel like I'm finally home. Your friendships are the best part of this writing journey.

Iram Aslam Weiser, without you, I would not have attempted to write fiction. Your mark is on this book, and I am forever thankful for you and your friendship.

Rebecca Petruck, you are truly a plot wizard! Thank you for choosing me for Pitch Wars, for teaching me so much about writing middle grade and the publishing world, and for being one of the kindest and most generous people I've ever met. My favorite people in the world are those who know how to laugh. I love laughing with you. I am most grateful for your friendship.

Lani Frank, thank you for helping me cut this manuscript and for making this book infinitely better. Your feedback made me a better writer. And your kindness, wit, and late-night text sessions helped me feel less alone in the process.

Hena Khan, your keen editorial feedback was priceless. I'm so grateful to have had you as my Highlights Muslim Storytellers mentor. You are truly a brilliant writer and a trailblazer for Muslim authors in this space. We are so grateful to you for leading the way and bringing us along. I hope to one day do the same, Insha'Allah.

Catherine Egan, you've been such a big part of this book's journey, from the very beginning, when it was about something else entirely. Thank you for your endless encouragement and guidance. Your editorial eye and infectious enthusiasm helped me fall in love with my book when I was in the pits of doubt. I am so grateful for your help and your friendship and that you are part of my New Haven family.

To my wise, inspiring, awesome Debut Sistars—Autumn Allen, Khadijah Van Brackle, Kaija Langley, and Jan Thomas. I love our little group, with our big stories and lofty dreams. Thank you for all your advice and support along the way. I'm so blessed to be on this journey with you all. Onward!

I found out that *Tagging Freedom* sold in the first few months of the Highlights Muslim Storytellers fellowship. Thank you to the Highlights Foundation and the Doris Duke Foundation for creating a safe space for us and for elevating and supporting our stories. This book is a better book because of this fellowship. A special thank-you to the mentors who gave us their time and shared their wisdom, especially Hena Khan, Jamilah Thompkins-Bigelow and S. K. Ali.

And to the Muslim Storytellers, I am in awe of each of you and feel so blessed to be a part of this talented cohort. Alhamdulillah.

And thank you to friends and critique partners who read this manuscript at different points along the way. My Syrian kidlit sisters—Shifa Safadi, Nadine Presley—I can't wait to hold your books in my hands and to read them with my children one day, Insha'allah. Bayan al-Talib, Kaisa Ehresman, Salam Zahr, Alana Dlubak, Robert Greene, Zareena Grewal, and Prathap Soori, thank you for reading and giving me your feedback. I am eternally grateful.

Saadia Faruqi, thank you for being such a strong champion of #ownvoices within our diverse Muslim community and for generously agreeing to read my entire manuscript and provide feedback after a quick online chat. I didn't know people like you existed.

And to Aya Khalil and Salam Zahr, my Arab writers who persist and persist and persist. Thank you for always making me laugh. You are the best part of this journey.

Intisar Rabb and Uzma Saiduddin Yasin, thank you for always supporting me; for being my home away from home; and for always keeping it real. I love you both so much.

To Zareena Grewal, Khadijah Gurnah, et al. (the New Haven pod); Teresa Chahine, Shahira Malm, Laila Kassis, and Mona Mowafi (my Arab sisters)—I am inspired by you all and love you all so much.

To the committee—Lina Sinjab, Aliya Mawani, Ana Escrogima, Gufran Nadaf, and Maan Abdul-Salam—I think of our Syria years often.

I attended my first protest in Syria in 2004 as a journalist. I had never seen anything like it, and, back then, I could have never imagined that a revolution was just a few years away. Yassin Haj-Saleh, you and Samira Khalil introduced me to a world that I never knew existed in Syria. You welcomed me into your home and opened up a new world to me—both as a journalist, and as a Syrian-American. The past decade has shown us the heartbreak that lives alongside such hope—and nobody has experienced that more than the activists who believed that change was possible and who believed that Syrians deserved more. You, Samira, Razan Zaitouneh, and so many others represent the Syria that we still dream about.

To my family. Nadia and Leila, I love you both so much. I couldn't ask for better sisters. Mama and Baba, your love and support are my foundation. Thank you for loving us unconditionally; for making Syria a part of our home, even when it was so far away; and for teaching us, from an early age, to care about the world around us. And for always reminding us to laugh.

Samia and Nadeem, may you always find the strength and courage to stand up for justice and may your voices always ring loud and clear. Thank you for being my biggest cheerleaders. You are the reason I write. You are my light.

And to Hani. My best friend. My partner. Albey. Thank you for letting me cry on your shoulder, and for then always making me laugh, often in the same hour. Sometimes at the same time. You didn't know what marrying a writer would look like, but you handle it all with grace. I love you.

And, finally, this book is a tribute to the memory of Hamza al-Khateeb and to the many Syrian children who lost their lives or who had to leave their homes. We hold you in our hearts and we pray for a better future for all of Syria's children.